The

"They intend to

Pythia gave a stifled exclamation of horror.

She was almost breathless as she reached the room where the King, her new husband, was.

There, stretched out on a divan, was the most beautiful woman Pythia had ever seen.

The woman and the King were speaking French and did not realise Pythia was standing in the doorway.

She took two hesitant steps forward before the King exclaimed:

"What are you doing here?"

For a moment Pythia did not know what to reply.

Then, as if she was being prompted, the words came to her lips. . . .

A Camfield Novel of Love
by Barbara Cartland

———

"Barbara Cartland's novels are all distinguished by their intelligence, good sense, and good nature . . ."
—ROMANTIC TIMES

"Who could give better advice on how to keep your romance going strong than the world's most famous romance novelist, Barbara Cartland?"
—THE STAR

Camfield Place,
Hatfield
Hertfordshire,
England

Dearest Reader,

Camfield Novels of Love mark a very exciting era of my books with Jove. They have already published nearly two hundred of my titles since they became my first publisher in America, and now all my original paperback romances in the future will be published exclusively by them.

As you already know, Camfield Place in Hertfordshire is my home, which originally existed in 1275, but was rebuilt in 1867 by the grandfather of Beatrix Potter.

It was here in the lovely house, with the best view in the county, that she wrote *The Tale of Peter Rabbit*. Mr. McGregor's garden is exactly as she described it. The door in the wall that the fat little rabbit could not squeeze underneath and the goldfish pool where the white cat sat twitching its tail are still there.

I had Camfield Place blessed when I came here in 1950 and was so happy with my husband until he died, and now with my children and grandchildren, that I know the atmosphere is filled with love and we have all been very lucky.

It is easy here to write of love and I know you will enjoy the Camfield Novels of Love. Their plots are definitely exciting and the covers very romantic. They come to you, like all my books, with love.

Bless you,

CAMFIELD NOVELS OF LOVE
by *Barbara Cartland*

Other Books by *Barbara Cartland*

A NEW CAMFIELD NOVEL OF LOVE BY

BARBARA CARTLAND

The Queen Saves the King

JOVE BOOKS, NEW YORK

THE QUEEN SAVES THE KING

A Jove Book / published by arrangement with
the author

PRINTING HISTORY
Jove edition / January 1991

ISBN: 0-515-10497-3

Jove Books are published by The Berkley Publishing Group,
200 Madison Avenue, New York, New York 10016.
The name "JOVE" and the "J" logo
are trademarks belonging to Jove Publications, Inc.

PRINTED IN THE UNITED STATES OF AMERICA

10 9 8 7 6 5 4 3 2 1

Author's Note

THE situation described in this book in 1874 merely anticipated what happened the next year when Serbia declared War on Turkey and thousands of Russian Volunteers poured into Leningrad.

The Tsar Alexander had no wish for a War, but he was pushed into it by the Empress and her ladies, who fluttered about referring endlessly to Russia's Holy mission.

Finally the Tsar began to believe it, and in November 1876, the Grand Duke Nicholas started his march towards Constantinople.

The conflict lasted for nine months and took a terrible toll of life. In one battle alone the Russians lost 25,000 men without gaining an inch of ground.

The army was, however, within six miles of Constantinople when Queen Victoria, who was frantically agitated by this time, suddenly persuaded the Cabinet to send Admiral Hornby with six iron-clad Battle ships to move into the Dardanelles to remind Russia that Britain would not stand aside for ever.

Russia was obliged to retreat and a Treaty was hammered out at the Congress of Berlin.

What was more important than anything else was that Russia had been denied access to the Mediterranean which she had hoped to reach through Bulgaria's back door.

The Queen Saves the King

chapter one

1874

"WHAT the hell do they want?"

King Alexius of Vultarnia spoke angrily.

He was just about to go riding when his *Aide-de-Camp* informed him that the Prime Minister and three other gentlemen had called to see him on urgent business.

"I have no idea, Your Majesty," the *Aide-de-Camp* replied apologetically, "but the Prime Minister would not have come at this hour had it not been of importance."

"Importance! Importance!" the King exclaimed testily. "Everything is important to them except what interests me!"

He had been looking forward this morning to riding a new horse he had recently acquired.

It was a magnificent stallion which had been bred in Hungary.

The King had already enjoyed numerous tussles with the spirited animal, which was beginning to realise that he had met his master.

"I am damned if I give them long," the King said.

As he spoke he knew he was being optimistic.

He knew how long-winded the Prime Minister could be, while most Members of the Cabinet were even worse.

As he was young compared to them, he found these sessions in which he had to listen to speech after speech extremely boring.

Vultarnia was a small country bordered by Montenegro and Albania and on the South by Macedonia.

It was beautiful, poor, and undeveloped.

The King had only recently come to the throne after his father died at nearly seventy.

He had so far few ideas of what he should do about his country.

He was, in fact, slightly resentful at having had to come back to his own country when he was enjoying himself travelling in Europe.

He had spent a considerable amount of time in Paris.

An extremely handsome man, women found him irresistible, which was exactly how he found them.

Now he walked out of the room without another word to his *Aide-de-Camp*.

He strode along the passage, all the more irritated to see that the sun was shining through the windows.

The Palace was a large building which had been added to over the centuries and had acquired a rambling charm of its own.

The King's mother had improved the main rooms with chandeliers from Venice and inlaid furniture from France.

She had also employed a number of local craftsmen.

They had carved and painted in the traditional manner which was prevalent all over the Balkans.

The King went down an impressive staircase.

In the hall a flunkey ran ahead to open the door into the Council Chamber.

This was actually a far more attractive room than its name suggested.

The King's mother had added pillars in front of what had previously been long bare walls.

Italian artists had embellished the ceiling with a painting of Venus rising from the foam.

The chairs on each side of the oblong table were upholstered in a deep shade of pink which matched the curtains.

Now the room seemed uncomfortably large for the four men who waited at the head of the table.

They rose as the King entered.

He saw, as he had expected, his Prime Minister, the Lord Chancellor, and the Secretary of State for Foreign Affairs.

The fourth man was a stranger.

As the King reached his chair, which was almost like a throne at the head of the table, he said:

"Good morning, Gentlemen!"

"Good morning, Your Majesty," the Statesmen answered.

The King seated himself as the Prime Minister said:

"May I, Your Majesty, present Count Kojotski, who arrived home last night."

The King smiled.

Now he knew who the stranger was.

He had been told some months before that a man who was half-Russian and half-Vultarnian was helping the Secretary of State for Foreign Affairs.

His mother, who had married a Russian nobleman, was a Vultarnian by birth.

But the Count lived in Tolskari, the capital of Vultarnia, where many of his relatives lived.

At the same time, he often went back to Russia.

His Majesty was aware that the Secretary of State had been using him to all intents and purposes as a spy.

"The Count has come to the Palace this morning, Your Majesty," the Prime Minister said in his pompous voice, "to inform you of what we think is a very dangerous situation which will affect not only our country but the whole of the Balkans."

The King raised his eye-brows.

He was wondering what information from Russia could possibly be of such importance to Vultarnia.

A number of people, he knew, were highly suspicious of Russia.

The King himself, however, had always thought they were "making a mountain out of a mole-hill."

Now, as the Prime Minister glanced at him, Count Kojotski said:

"I think you are aware, Your Majesty, that Russia has grown increasingly envious of Bismarck's unification of Germany."

"I have heard that," the King said, "but I cannot imagine what they can do about it."

"The argument in St. Petersburg," the Count said, "is simply if Prussia could form all the German States and the German peoples into a mighty Empire, why should not Russia do the same?"

The King stared at the Count. Then he asked:

"How do they propose to do that?"

"The question being asked," the Count replied, "is why should not Russia gather together under her auspices all the Slavs in the Balkans and in European Turkey."

The King was silent.

He remembered now that he had, in fact, heard this suggestion before, but had not taken it seriously.

As he did not speak, the Count continued:

"I returned from St. Petersburg yesterday and I thought it only right to inform the Prime Minister that this aim is now being openly talked about in the Palace and in every Ministry in both St. Petersburg and Moscow."

The Foreign Secretary leant across the table to say:

"Even before the Count returned, Sire, I was told

this was happening, but I waited to have it confirmed."

"The Empress," the Count went on, "sees it as a religious crusade. She wants to bring back the Church of Santa Sophia to its rightful Orthodoxy and make Constantinople the greatest City in Christendom."

The King thought this was what she might well be expected to want.

"And the Tsarevitch, for his part, Sire," the Count continued, "is determined to open the Straits to Russian ships and to acquire thousands of square miles of new territory in the Balkans."

"It seems impossible," the King murmured.

At the same time, because he knew that this was an age-old dream of the Russians, he could understand how much the idea appealed to them.

"Have you any reason to believe," he asked, "that things are going further than the mere chatter of tongues?"

"Every reason, Sire," the Count replied. "The Emperor's brother, the Grand Duke Nicholas, is already mobilising troops into a large Army with which he intends to invade the Balkans and march on Constantinople."

"You are sure of this?" the King asked.

"Completely sure, Sire," the Count replied. "Many of my friends in Russia are talking of joining the Army, and quite a number of them have already done so. They think there will be little opposition and they will undoubtedly start their offensive within a few months."

"I can hardly believe it!" the King exclaimed.

"But if it is true, what can we, a very small country, do about it?"

"That is the question, Your Majesty, which has kept me awake all night," the Prime Minister said. "This morning, after a long talk with the Foreign Secretary, and, of course, the Lord Chancellor, I am convinced there is one action we can take which could protect our independence better than any other."

"What is that?" the King asked.

"That Your Majesty should request Queen Victoria of England to provide you with a wife."

The King stared at the Prime Minister in sheer astonishment.

He had not thought of marrying; in fact, he had no intention of doing so.

He was at the moment having a wild and passionate affair with a very attractive and extremely exotic Russian Countess.

She had come to Vultarnia after her husband's death.

The King had met her by chance and been immediately attracted by her.

She was certainly different in every way from the Vultarnian women.

They were pretty, but definitely countrified compared with the women who had amused him in other Cities, especially Paris.

The Countess had spent a great deal of her time in France because her husband had been a Diplomat.

Her excuse for coming to Tolskari was that she had many friends in Vultarnia, which was true.

But from the moment she met the King she

7

appeared to have little further use for them.

At first they had difficulty in meeting, until he invited her to stay in the Palace.

One wing was used as a guest-house and was regularly filled with visitors from other parts of the world.

There was no question of her not being discreetly chaperoned.

The fact that she moved about the Palace had nothing to do with anyone outside the Royal precincts.

The King found her very desirable.

He could not help thinking when the Count was decrying Russia that the first thing the Prime Minister would do would be to hint that he should not be so intimate with the Countess.

He had, however, no intention of letting his Statesmen interfere in his private affairs.

But he had never imagined that so soon after he had become their Monarch they would demand that he give them a Queen.

Now it flashed through his mind that this was what he might have anticipated.

Because he was *au fait* with foreign affairs, he would understand exactly the way their minds worked.

Queen Victoria had placed her relatives—and there were a great number of them—on at least a dozen Royal and Princely thrones.

When he had been in France he had heard her referred to as "The Match-maker of Europe."

Even so, he had not expected to be caught up in her web of intrigue.

Britain had become undoubtedly the strongest

and the most feared power in the whole world.

The King was aware that if Russia was afraid of anyone, it would be of Britain.

"I have always heard," the Foreign Secretary was saying, "that Her Majesty Queen Victoria is suspicious of Russian ambitions."

The King thought that was very likely true.

"It was with great reluctance," the Foreign Secretary went on, "that Her Majesty agreed to the marriage of the Duke of Edinburgh to the Grand Duchess Maria of Russia."

As this had taken place only last year, the King remembered the occasion.

He had, however, not been present at the ceremony.

"What we are asking Your Majesty," the Prime Minister said, "is your agreement to send an Envoy immediately to Britain to ask Her Majesty Queen Victoria to suggest a suitable wife for Your Majesty and for the wedding to take place as soon as possible."

The King stiffened.

With difficulty he checked the words which came instinctively to his lips.

He wanted to say that he had no intention of marrying anyone, least of all some unattractive, heavily-built young Englishwoman with whom he would have nothing in common.

He was not an admirer of Englishwomen as a whole.

He thought they compared very unfavourably with the grace, wit, and the irresistible fascination of the French.

9

In fact, he classed the English, the Dutch, and the Germans as boring in the extreme.

The French, the Greeks, and the Italians were very different.

He had also had a Spanish mistress at one time whom he had found alluring.

Unfortunately, her passion for eating everything swimming in fat had brought the liaison to an end.

He tried to think of someone other than an Englishwoman who would ensure the safety of his country, anyone to prevent him having to be bored with, as he expressed it quietly to himself, "going to bed with the Union Jack."

"You do understand, Your Majesty," the Secretary of State was saying earnestly, "that the only way we can preserve our freedom and avoid coming under Russian domination would be to have a relative of Queen Victoria on the throne."

"Are you quite sure the Russians would respect Her Majesty's wishes when she is so far away!" the King asked sarcastically.

"The British Navy is the largest, best equipped navy in the world," the Foreign Secretary replied, "and I am quite certain that if the Russians really try to take Constantinople, Britain will intervene."

The King had to admit this was likely.

He was therefore silent while the Lord Chancellor said, speaking for the first time:

"I understand, Sire, this has all come as something of a shock, but we all of us agree, and I know Parliament will too, that it is the only solution, the only safeguard we have against a Russian invasion."

The King could not answer this.

He knew that with the very small Army they had, a big power like Russia could defeat it at the first encounter.

Too late he wished that at the very beginning of his reign he had insisted on strengthening their defences.

He should have spent a large amount of money on armaments.

Even so, he doubted if that would prove at all effective.

Every nerve in his body cried out against being tied down to some bossy Englishwoman.

She would be well aware that she was doing him a favour in being a life-line for his Kingdom.

Because the idea not only disturbed but repelled him, he pushed back his chair.

He walked across the room to stand at one of the windows looking out.

The Palace was high above the City.

He could see the towers and spires of the Churches, the dome of the House of Parliament.

Through the trees there was an occasional glimpse of horses and vehicles moving down the main road.

In the distance were the mountains, their peaks still white with snow.

The sun was shining on the red tiles of the roofs of the houses.

It glittered on the river which divided the City and flowed from it into a fertile valley where peasants tended the crops.

It was very picturesque, very peaceful, and very beautiful.

Because it was his and he reigned over it, the King, although he did not say so, was very proud of his country.

There had been no revolutions as there had been in many other Balkan countries.

His crown had descended from father to son for five generations.

He had always known that one day his son would follow him.

What he had not envisaged was having an English wife.

How could he bear to have as a wife a woman who bored him.

She would undoubtedly curtail the amusements he had enjoyed ever since he had come home to take his father's place.

Although he had his back to them, he had a feeling that his Statesmen were looking at each other knowingly.

They were thinking that he would have to send his Russian mistress away.

As far as they were concerned, the sooner the better.

Of course he had been aware that they disliked his being always with a woman from another country, whether it was Russia or anywhere else.

Now, when the threat came definitely from Russia, Natasha would have to go.

"I am damned if I will let them dictate to me!" the King told himself.

At the same time, he felt as if Queen Victoria's hand were reaching out towards him.

Already, like a helpless fly, he was caught in the

spider's web, and there was no chance of escape.

That was the right phrase.

"No chance of escape!"

He repeated it to himself.

He was, in fact, being crushed between two great forces, Russia on his right, Britain on his left.

It made him furiously angry to know there was nothing he could do about it.

He walked back to the table.

The Statesmen rose to their feet and he looked at the Foreign Secretary.

"Very well," he said, "you leave me no option. Send your Envoy to Queen Victoria!"

He did not wait for a reply, but walked from the room.

Although he told himself it was childish, he slammed the door behind him.

* * *

Her Majesty Queen Victoria received Mr. Benjamin Disraeli with pleasure.

She had a fondness for him. It was only equalled by what had amounted to her adoration of Lord Melbourne when she had first come to the throne.

Mr. Disraeli flattered her.

He actually wooed her with flowers and compliments that she had never enjoyed from any of her other Prime Ministers.

This morning, with the sun coming through the windows of the Castle, he looked more fantastic than usual.

As he lifted the Queen's hand to his lips, she

smiled at him almost girlishly.

She noticed he had brought with him the Earl of Derby, who was Secretary of State for Foreign Affairs, also Viscount Branbrook, the Secretary of State for War.

When she had seated herself, the gentlemen stood in front of her.

"We have come, Your Majesty," the Prime Minister said, "to ask as usual for your help and wisdom in a difficult situation which has actually already been brought to Your Majesty's attention."

"In that case, Prime Minister," Queen Victoria remarked, "I am sure it concerns Russia!"

Mr. Disraeli smiled and exclaimed:

"Has Your Majesty ever been wrong? Who else has such a knowledge of the dangerous situation which seems likely to confront us in Europe?"

"What has happened now?" the Queen asked.

"Our Agents have been telling us for some time, as Your Majesty knows," Mr. Disraeli answered, "of Russia's ambition to overrun the Balkans and European Turkey. They wish to establish themselves as a power as great as Germany and, of course, as Britain."

"And have you any sensible ideas as to how we can stop them from doing that?" the Queen asked.

"We are, of course, attending very closely to what is happening," Mr. Disraeli replied. "Today we have received a request from His Majesty King Alexius of Vultarnia, which has come as a welcome surprise."

"What is that?" the Queen enquired.

"It is to beg Your Majesty, in your wisdom and

awareness of Vultarnia's precarious position, to provide His Majesty with a British bride."

The Queen nodded.

"I can understand the King's reasoning. I suppose we have a Royal Princess who would be able to undertake what will undoubtedly prove a difficult task."

There was a silence.

The three Statesmen were thinking there was no need to tell the Queen that King Alexius had the reputation of being a Roué.

He had certainly as a young man, "sown his wild oats" in France as well as in other parts of Europe.

At the same time, he was now over thirty.

Since he came to the throne he must be thinking of settling down, the Queen imagined.

Lord Derby, however, had learned from one of his agents that the King was at the moment very occupied with a Russian Countess.

She was actually a guest in his Palace.

Almost as if the Queen were able to read his thoughts, she said:

"What we really need is a sensible young woman of perhaps twenty-eight or twenty-nine who could put forward British ideas of how a country should be run rather than leaving it to Muslims, who do not seem to know their business."

"Of course Your Majesty is entirely right," Mr. Disraeli said. "The difficulty is that we can, none of us, and we have tried, think of anyone we can recommend to Your Majesty's notice."

"There must be someone!" the Queen said sharply. "Heaven knows, I have enough relatives, and where I have placed them on a number of thrones they have been successful."

"They have indeed, Ma'am," Lord Derby said, "and I cannot tell you how grateful I am to Your Majesty for your understanding of what is a difficult task for a Foreign Secretary."

The Queen laughed.

"I can well believe that, Lord Derby."

There was silence, and she said:

"Well? I am waiting for your suggestions."

"We are praying, Your Majesty," Mr. Disraeli said, "that that is what you can give us."

"There must be someone!" the Queen said again.

It was then that Lord Cranbrook said:

"I have just remembered, Your Majesty, that a distant relative, Prince Lucian of Seriphos, married the daughter of the Earl of O'Kelly, who was a friend of my father's."

The Queen's eyes lit up.

"Yes, of course! Princess Aileen. After her husband's death, I gave her a house on the edge of the Park."

"Your Majesty's memory is amazing, as usual," Mr. Disraeli said. "And unless I am mistaken, the Princess Aileen has a daughter."

"She has," the Queen replied. "Her name is Princess Erina, which I have always thought was an unsuitable name, although it is Irish."

No one spoke, then after a moment Mr. Disraeli said:

"Will Your Majesty graciously speak to Princess Aileen? If we are correct in our interpretation of the reports which are coming through from our agents in Russia, the sooner the marriage takes place the better!"

"Can it really be as bad as that?" the Queen asked.

"There is no doubt, Your Majesty," Lord Derby replied, "that the Grand Duke Nicholas is mobilising a large Army. As Russia is so vast a country, this will take time, but there is no possible reason why he should require so many men unless he intends, as we expect, to invade the Balkans."

The Queen sighed.

"We shall have great difficulty in preventing them from doing that."

She paused before she added beneath her breath:

"I have always believed it would be a question of either Russian or British supremacy in the world."

Mr. Disraeli sighed before he said:

"I am afraid Your Majesty will have difficulty in making the Cabinet believe it is a real danger."

"Then we shall have to convince them," the Queen said firmly.

Then, as if she had decided to put first things first, she said:

"I will send for Princess Aileen to call on me this afternoon, and I will then, Prime Minister, inform you exactly when Princess Erina can leave for Vultarnia."

"I can only thank you, Ma'am, from the bottom of my heart," Mr. Disraeli said. "I knew I could rely on you, and you have never failed me."

He smiled at her and she smiled back as if they understood each other.

They were both aware of the problem of persuading the Cabinet and Parliament of the difficulties and dangers which they saw so clearly.

Mr. Disraeli and the Ministers left.

When the Queen was alone, she sat for a long time with a frown between her eyes.

She was trying to think if there was anyone more suitable for the post she had to offer than the daughter of Princess Aileen and the late Prince Lucian.

Her mind, which was very sharp, ranged over her relations one by one.

Just as Mr. Disraeli and Lord Derby had done, she realised there was, in fact, no other Princess.

The Queen could not remember even seeing Erina.

Now she thought she had in fact been rather remiss in not inviting the widowed Princess Aileen to any of the functions at Windsor Castle.

Prince Lucian of Seriphos, which was a small island in the Aegean Archipelago, had visited Ireland.

He had wished to enjoy the hunting there which was known in Europe to be exciting and more demanding than anywhere else.

While he was there he met the elder daughter of the Earl of O'Kelly and lost his heart.

Princess Aileen was not only a very good rider, she was breathtakingly lovely.

She had not met many young men since she had grown up.

The Greek prince, with his classical features, had a charm she had never encountered before.

He swept her off her feet.

They were married and went to live on Seriphos in what no one could call very luxurious surroundings.

At the same time, they had been supremely happy.

Sixteen years later the Prince was killed in one of the uprisings which were continually taking place in Greece.

Broken-hearted, Princess Aileen came back to England with their daughter, aged fifteen.

While she was away her father had died.

The new Earl of O'Kelly, a distant Cousin, made no offer of hospitality.

In fact, he made it clear there was no particular welcome for the Princess in Ireland.

She had, therefore, gone to Queen Victoria for assistance.

She had been allowed to marry Prince Lucian simply because the Earls of O'Kelly were descended from the Irish Kings.

She was also a distant cousin of Queen Victoria herself.

It had been impossible at that particular time for her to be given a Grace and Favour apartment at Hampton Court.

The Queen had therefore offered her a house, and it was little more than a cottage, on the outskirts of Windsor Park.

She also made her a small allowance which was just enough to keep her and her daughter from starvation.

After the revolt in Seriphos was over, money occasionally trickled in small amounts to England.

Princess Aileen had to count every penny, and in the last year or so she had not been in very good health.

The Queen despatched one of her Gentlemen-in-Waiting to the thatched cottage where Princess Aileen lived.

When he had left, Her Majesty took her Family Tree from a drawer in the desk of her Sitting-Room.

She studied it carefully.

She was still hoping that by a miracle she would find someone more suitable for the dashing and undoubtedly very sophisticated King of Vultarnia.

She scrutinised every name and turned up certain reference books to make sure she had not overlooked some near relative.

But it came back to one thing, and one thing only.

The only eligible Princess was Erina who, according to the records, was only nineteen years old.

If the British Flag was to prove a symbol of safety for Vultarnia, the Princess was the only person who could wave it.

The Queen replaced her Family Tree in its drawer.

She told herself again she had been remiss in not having taken more interest in Princess Aileen and her daughter.

Until now she had thought them of little importance.

With so many duties to perform, it had not occurred to her to supervise the girl's education.

She had not thought of her as being an eligible match for a Monarch in Europe should the occasion arise.

'It is my own fault!' the Queen thought. 'And it is now too late to do anything about it.'

She remembered that tomorrow she was leaving for France on one of her holidays that she greatly enjoyed.

She had first visited France in 1843, thirty-one years before.

It had been an adventure, apart from the fact that the beloved Prince Consort had been at her side.

She was prepared to go anywhere in the world if it was with him.

Now, except for members of her household, she went alone.

She travelled in the Royal Yacht to France and was looking forward to being at sea again.

She had known, without Mr. Disraeli telling her, that if Russia was mobilising her Armies it was important for the King of Vultarnia to be married as quickly as possible.

"There is nothing I can do about the girl," she said angrily, "and after all, I was only eighteen when I came to the throne."

She thought of what a success she had been, and how powerful she had become over the years.

She sat down at her writing-desk.

She entered in her Diary that the Prime Minister had come to ask for her assistance.

The problem had been solved, yet she could not help wondering what King Alexius would think about it.

chapter two

PYTHIA started preparing supper.

She was a far better cook than Erina.

Soon after she had come to live in the little thatched cottage, she had found that they enjoyed the food she prepared. She had taken over the cooking.

She did not mind because she had done it for her father and mother.

When she thought back of what fun it had been when they had eaten a meal cooked over a Gypsy's fire or in a peasant's cottage, she wanted to cry.

But tears would not bring back her parents.

She knew she had to show the courage which had been characteristic of her mother.

After Lady Aileen O'Kelly had married Prince Lucian of Seriphos, her father, the Earl, had hoped that his second daughter would make an equally impressive marriage.

He was not exactly a snob, but he was extremely proud of being descended from the Irish Kings.

It was therefore a bitter blow when after the birth of two daughters his wife could have no more children.

However, his two daughters, being extremely pretty, became the joy of his heart.

When Prince Lucian proposed to Aileen, he gave the union his whole-hearted blessing.

The Earl, of course, could have had no idea that one day in the not so distant future Prince Lucian would have to leave Seriphos and that the Royal connection with Seriphos would come to an end.

Aileen O'Kelly had been beautiful, and it was not surprising that her only child, Erina, should be beautiful too.

Erina was extremely striking with dark hair inherited from her father and blue eyes from her mother.

As she had dark lashes, the Irish called them "blue eyes put in with dirty fingers."

The Earl's second daughter, Clodagh, was also extremely pretty.

In fact, many people thought she was prettier than her sister.

There was only eighteen months in age between the two girls.

After the wedding was over and Prince Lucian took his bride to Greece, the Earl looked around for a suitable match for Clodagh.

There were quite a number of young men of distinguished birth in Ireland.

But their families were all impoverished and their Castles fell down.

The Earl, therefore, began to think it might be best for her to have a rich English husband.

Then the blow fell.

Clodagh fell madly in love with Patrick O'Connor, who lived only a few miles away from her home.

He was seven years older than she was and had been in England studying medicine.

Having gained a degree, he came back to Ireland to see his family and decide what he should do next.

When he met Lady Clodagh he knew the only thing he wanted was to make her his wife.

They were obviously wildly and irrevocably infatuated with each other.

The Earl knew it would be quite useless for him to refuse to allow them to become engaged.

He merely said quietly:

"It will be a long engagement until Patrick can settle down in a practise—unless, of course, you are going to live on air!"

"We are going to see the world," Patrick replied.

"How do you intend to do that?" the Earl asked in surprise.

"I have worked it all out," Patrick answered. "I have no intention of burying myself and Clodagh in some stuffy little village where I shall tend the old and the maimed and occasionally set the leg of some boy who has fallen out of a tree when stacking apples."

The Earl was listening as Patrick went on:

"All I ask is at least to have my fares paid to the places where I wish to go. So I have approached the Missionary Society."

"The Missionary Society?" the Earl asked. "What can they do for you?"

"Everything I want," Patrick answered. "They are desperately short of Missionaries who have any medical skills."

"You intend to be a Priest?" the Earl said incredulously.

Patrick shook his head.

"I can hardly be that and marry Clodagh! No, I have talked to them and they are quite prepared to send me abroad, calling me a Medical Missionary. I shall be a Lay Preacher, which does not require clerical training."

"I do not believe it!" the Earl said.

"You must understand, My Lord," Patrick went on, "that Clodagh and I will go to places we have read about and longed to see. I can think of no other way to get there unless we swim!"

The Earl did not laugh at the joke. He merely said:

"I think you are crazy!"

"If we find it does not work out," Patrick said, "we can always come home. But I would not mind betting all the money I do not have that it will be a fantastic and delightful adventure."

That was exactly what it turned out to be.

As soon as they were married, Patrick and Clodagh set off in a cargo-boat which carried them first to Greece.

They stayed with Princess Aileen and found she was as happy with her Prince as they were.

Because Patrick had always longed, of all countries, to visit Greece, they stayed there for a year.

They explored the islands, Athens, the country beyond the City, and ended up in Delphi.

Pythia was born in a small wooden hut not far from where the Temple of Apollo had once stood.

She was delivered by her father, who said it was the most exciting experience of his life.

After she was born, he carried her in his arms amongst the ruins of what had been the great Temple and the shrines of other Greek gods.

He looked up at the shining cliffs and down into the valley.

It was there that Apollo had once leaped ashore to declare to the gods that everything he could see from where he stood was his.

Because he was not only the god of Light, but of Good Taste, he had chosen to own the loveliest place in Greece.

After the great Temple was built in his honour, thousands of pilgrims came every year to the little port of Chrisa.

They worshipped him and heard from the Priests the latest utterance of the Oracle.

It was her father who had told Pythia when she was old enough how she had received her name.

"Somewhere near the great Temple of Apollo there was a cave," he said, "where the Priestess, who was called Pythia, sat on a bronze tripod."

"Was she beautiful, Papa?" Pythia asked.

"I am sure she was as beautiful as you, my darling," Patrick O'Connor answered, "but the Pythia obviously changed from time to time because the Oracle was consulted at Delphi for more than a thousand years."

"And what did she do?" Pythia asked.

"She went into a trance and her incoherent utterances which were inspired by the god were interpreted by the Priests and recast in metrical verses. In this form answers were given to the suppliants who came to Delphi from the four corners of the earth."

"She must have been very proud."

"I am sure she was, and she was, of course, trained in the Priesthood—the only woman allowed into the Temple of Apollo."

"So that is why you called me Pythia!"

"As I held you in my arms," Patrick O'Connor answered, "I knew that was your name. Because I am a Celt I have a perception which is not accorded to many people."

He paused a moment and then went on:

"One day you will hold a very special place in the world and you will need the help of the spirits and gods who are still left in Delphi."

His voice deepened as he went on:

"I held you up and said to Apollo:

" 'Touch this child with your light, make her see with her eyes, hear with her ears, and speak with her lips the wisdom, the beauty, and light which comes from you. Let her in your name show the way for others who are not so blessed.' "

Pythia had given a little cry.

"Oh, Papa, that was a lovely prayer, and I am sure Apollo heard it."

"Of course he did!" Patrick O'Connor replied. "And you are just as lovely, my darling, as I wanted you to be."

That certainly was true.

Pythia had a strange, spiritual loveliness which made her different from other girls of her age.

Her hair was fair, very fair, the gold of the dawn when it first appears in the sky.

Her eyes were blue like her mother's and her eye-lashes were darker than her hair.

She was smaller than her cousin Erina, very slim and graceful.

To her father she had always exemplified Aphrodite, the goddess of Love.

Love was so much a part of Patrick O'Connor's life that he transmitted it to everyone wherever he went.

As they travelled about the Balkans they made many strange friends.

Patrick practised his medical skills on people of many nationalities.

They took a particularly long journey to Romania the Summer before the tragedy which changed Pythia's life.

She loved the great romantic country with its mountains and lakes, its rivers and wild valleys.

Pythia, like her mother, loved the animals they found everywhere.

There were the chamois in the mountains, where they also saw the bearded eagles.

In the forests there were the wild cats, bears, lynx, and stags.

There was also a huge variety of birds.

From Romania they travelled across Serbia.

After spending some time with the people there with whom her father had a close rapport, they moved on again into Macedonia.

Having spent her life in the Balkans, Pythia found it easy to talk all their languages.

It was his Irish blood and his Celtish intuition which made Patrick understand them all.

However complicated their problems, he could help and comfort those who sought him out.

He had, however, decided, after travelling such long distances over mountains and plains, along rivers and lakes, that they would now move to somewhere more civilised.

Although he did not say so, he felt it was time his beautiful daughter should meet some people of their own class.

He had friends in Italy who he knew would welcome them.

When they reached Montenegro they were unfortunately very short of money.

It took them a little time to find a cargo-ship, which was the cheapest way to travel to Italy.

The passage was cheap because the cargo was not a large one and the ship was very old.

Tragically, however, as they sailed into the Adriatic Sea a tempest rose which almost lifted the ship out of the water.

The Captain decided to try to return to Port.

It was, however, too late.

In the storm, which was a very fierce one, the ship literally seemed to fall to pieces.

Pythia was rescued by a sailor who kept her afloat.

Somehow, by what seemed later to be a miracle, they reached dry land.

Practically everybody else on board was drowned.

The ship itself foundered, and what was left of it was dashed against the rocks.

Pythia was sent back to England under the auspices of the British Embassy at Cetinje, the Capital of Montenegro.

The journey took a long time, but eventually she found her Aunt in Windsor Park.

Princess Aileen welcomed Pythia and wept when she heard how her sister had perished.

She and Erina were already finding it very difficult to make ends meet on the very small amount of money they had.

But, of course, she was ready to share everything they possessed with her orphaned niece.

Because she had loved her sister, she could hardly believe that she would never see her again or hear from her on her travels as she had over the years they had been apart.

"Mama talked about you so often, Aunt Aileen," Pythia said, "and it is very exciting for me to find I have a Cousin who is only a little older than I am."

Princess Aileen was delighted that the two girls became such friends.

At the same time, she wondered at night what

would become of them in the future.

She herself was not at all well.

She had suffered the last three winters from arthritis in her legs and back.

The weather had been extremely cold, and they could not afford to buy enough fuel for the fires.

The house was therefore cold and damp, but she was afraid to complain about it.

"I suppose really I am lucky to have a roof over my head," she told herself.

At the same time, she continually thought of the prosperous days she had enjoyed with Prince Lucian in Seriphos.

Then it was hard not to cry because she felt so helpless.

She often thought it was very unkind of Queen Victoria to ignore not only her, which really did not matter, but also Erina.

Never once had Erina been asked to any of the parties at Windsor Castle.

Now she had also Pythia, who was eighteen, to think of.

She was so lovely that when they went shopping, people in the streets stopped to stare at her.

A carriage drawn by two white horses had arrived at the thatched cottage.

The Princess was presented by a Gentleman-in-Waiting with a note.

It was from the Queen, asking Princess Aileen to visit her immediately on a matter of great importance.

The Princess could not imagine what had happened.

It flashed through her mind that perhaps after all this time the people of Seriphos had asked for her return.

Then she told herself that was very unlikely.

The horses were waiting.

As Erina was nowhere to be found, Pythia helped her Aunt into her best gown which she had not worn for several years.

Then she put on her smartest hat which was admittedly not very elegant.

"It is exciting for you, Aunt, going to Windsor Castle!" Pythia said. "Do try to remember everything you see and everyone you meet so that you can tell us about it this evening."

"I will certainly do that," the Princess agreed. "At the same time, I cannot imagine why Her Majesty wishes to see me."

She sounded so worried that Pythia knew she was very nervous.

"You must not be frightened, Aunt Aileen," she said. "When people used to tell us of somebody— a King or a Chieftain who was so overwhelming that people were terrified of him—Papa used to say 'After all, he is human and he will bleed if you prick him!'"

The Princess tried to laugh but failed.

Pythia knew that she was trembling as she got into the carriage.

She watched until the horses were out of sight and then went in search of her Cousin.

She knew she was somewhere in the vicinity, painting one of her watercolours which she hoped she could be able to sell.

33

"When I get a little better, Mama," she had said to the Princess, "I am going to take my pictures to the Art Shop in Windsor and ask them to sell them for me."

The Princess had been horrified.

"You cannot do that, Darling! Suppose the Queen heard about it?"

"If the Queen does not give us enough money to live on, we have to make some!" Erina said firmly. "I am tired of being poor, of never having a new gown or a hat that does not resemble a dilapidated birds' nest!"

The Princess had laughed, but there had been an expression of pain in her eyes.

As she drove towards Windsor Castle she remembered that conversation.

She wondered if she dared ask the Queen for just a little more money for the two girls.

Her Majesty was not aware that Pythia also was living in the thatched cottage.

There had seemed no point in advising her of it, nor of telling any of the officials in the Castle that she had a guest staying with her.

She doubted whether if she did, one penny would be added to the meagre allowance she received every month.

Pythia looked amongst the trees for some sign of Erina, then returned to the house.

"I wonder where she has gone?" she mused.

She went into the kitchen to look for something different they might have for dinner.

There was practically nothing in the Larder.

She thought perhaps what remained of the rabbit that had been snared by a boy in the wood yesterday would make a stew.

Pythia had given him a few pennies for it and he had gone away to try to snare another.

She was quite certain that the Queen's gamekeepers would be furious if they knew.

But it would have been foolhardy to send the boy away and go hungry.

She started to make the stew more nourishing with the addition of vegetables which came from their small garden.

She and Erina tended it themselves, but they could not always afford the necessary seeds and plants.

As she cooked, Pythia was thinking of the delicious and strange meals she had eaten with her father and mother in all parts of the Balkans.

They had even eaten bear when they were in Romania.

Chamois also in Romania had been a luxury when roasted properly.

'I could do with a chamois now!' Pythia thought.

As she polished one of the saucepans she heard a carriage draw up outside and knew her aunt had returned.

She ran to the front door.

The Princess was being assisted from the carriage by a footman.

It was a somewhat difficult process because of her unsteady legs.

Pythia ran forward to help her on the other side.

With the aid of them both, the Princess

reached the front-door and thanked the man for his assistance.

"It's a pleasure, Your Highness," he said politely, sweeping off his cockaded hat.

The Princess smiled at him and Pythia helped her into the house.

They moved into a small Sitting-Room.

When the Princess was seated on the sofa Pythia asked:

"Is everything all right, Aunt Aileen? Her Majesty did not eat you up?"

"No . . . no . . . not at all! Her Majesty was very kind," the Princess replied. "But where is Erina? I want to tell you both the good news!"

As she spoke, the door into the Sitting-Room opened and the Princess Erina came in.

She was looking flushed and excited.

Pythia saw to her surprise that behind her there was a very handsome man.

He did not look English, and while she was wondering who it could be, Erina ran to her mother to say:

"Mama, I have brought someone to meet you."

The Princess looked up in surprise and Erina went on:

"May I present, Mama, Don Marcos Roca? He comes from Peru."

"How do you do!" the Princess said politely.

Don Marcos Roca bent over her hand before he said:

"It is a very great pleasure to meet Your Highness, and I have come to ask if you will do me the great honour of allowing your daughter to become my wife!"

Pythia gasped. The Princess just stared at Don Marcos Roca in sheer astonishment.

Erina went down on her knees beside her mother.

"You must forgive me, Mama, that I did not tell you before about Marcos. I met him only a week ago when I was painting a picture of the Castle, and I am afraid that I have met him every day since."

"Why did you not tell me about him?" the Princess asked gently.

Her daughter smiled.

"I was terrified that he would go away and forget about me, and because I wanted him so much to stay I was afraid to talk about him in case it was unlucky."

"I have loved Erina from the moment I first saw her," Marcos Roca interrupted, "and I knew then that all my dreams had come true. How can anyone be so lovely and not be just a part of my imagination?"

As he spoke his eyes met Erina's.

It was obvious to the two people watching that for a moment the world had stood still. There were only themselves in it.

The Princess looked at them in a somewhat bemused fashion.

Then she gave a little cry and said:

"If you are asking Erina to marry you, it is impossible—quite impossible!"

Marcos Roca stiffened.

"Impossible, Your Highness?"

Erina jumped to her feet.

"You cannot mean that, Mama! I love . . . Marcos, I love him with . . . all my . . . heart . . . and I know . . . he loves . . . me."

She went to his side as if for protection, and he put his arm round her.

"I am afraid, Your Highness," he said very respectfully, "that this has been a shock, but I assure you I will look after Erina and make her happy."

He paused a moment and then continued:

"My father is the Prime Minister of Peru and a very wealthy man. My whole family will, I know, welcome Erina from the moment they see her."

"Roca!" the Princess exclaimed. "Now I know who you are, and I think it must have been your father who stayed with us once on Seriphos."

Marcos Roca smiled and said:

"I know my father was in Greece ten or twelve years ago. He thought it one of the most beautiful places in the world."

"I remember him well," the Princess said. "I can see you bear a distinct likeness to him."

She paused.

Then in a very different tone she added:

"But . . . you cannot marry Erina! Her Majesty the Queen has . . . arranged for . . . her to marry . . . King Alexius of Vultarnia!"

For a moment there was complete silence in the room.

Then Erina cried:

"I do not believe it! When did the Queen tell you this?"

"She sent a carriage for me," the Princess answered, "and I have only just returned from the Castle. I could not imagine why she wanted to see me, but that was the reason."

"I will not marry . . . the King . . . I will . . . not!" Erina exclaimed. "I want to marry Marcos . . . I love him!"

She saw the expression on her mother's face and said:

"You have always told me that you married Papa, not because he was a Prince but because you fell in love. How . . . loving Marcos could I . . . marry some . . . strange man I have . . . never seen?"

The Peruvian took her by the shoulders and turned her round to face him.

"Do you mean that? Do you really mean it?"

"Of course I mean it!" Erina said. "I love you . . . and if you . . . leave me I shall want to . . . die!"

"That is what I feel about you," Marcos Roca said, "but you are quite certain you are making the right choice?"

"Completely and absolutely certain," Erina said.

For a moment they just stood looking at each other and it seemed to Pythia that their hearts reached out to become one.

Erina turned towards her mother.

"I am sorry, Mama," she said, "but you must tell the Queen that it is impossible for me to marry anyone but Marcos, and she will have to find another bride for the King!"

Princess Aileen clasped her hands together.

"Oh, darling, how can I go back to the Queen

with such a message? She did not ask me if you would marry the King."

She drew in her breath and went on:

"She simply told me that was what you were to do. Moreover, she added that there was nobody else."

"What do you mean . . . nobody else?" Erina enquired.

"Her Majesty said that she thought you were really too young and not capable of taking up such an important position at this particular moment of history, but you were the only unmarried and available relative she had."

She stopped speaking, and there was a little silence before she continued:

"Therefore, somewhat reluctantly, she had given her consent for you to leave within two weeks for Vultarnia."

The Princess's voice died away and Erina gave a scream.

"I will . . . not do it! I will . . . not! No-one can . . . force me to . . . marry anyone . . . even if he is . . . a King!"

"That is true," Marcos Roca agreed.

"It is not true in this country," the Princess said. "Erina has to marry whoever as her legal Guardian I choose for her, and if I fail in my duty, the Queen can make it a Royal Command!"

Erina hid her face against Marcos Roca's shoulder and burst into tears.

"I will not . . . I will . . . not marry . . . the King! Oh, Marcos . . . save me, I want to be . . . your wife!"

Holding her closely against him, the Peruvian said in a quiet voice to the Princess:

"Are you absolutely certain that you cannot persuade Her Majesty to change her mind?"

"I know she would not listen to me," the Princess answered helplessly. "I want above all things my daughter's happiness, but if we make the Queen angry, anything might happen."

She hesitated before she went on:

"She might turn me out of this house and then Pythia and I would have nowhere to go and no income."

"I would not let you starve," Marcos Roca said, "of that you can be sure, but there must be a solution."

Erina raised her head from his shoulder.

"I love you . . . oh, Marcos . . . I love you!" she said. "You are so clever . . . think of some way that . . . you can . . . save me!"

Her voice was pitiful and the tears were running down her cheeks.

Marcos drew her closely to him.

Then Erina gave a little cry.

"I have an idea!" she said.

They all looked at her and waited, and after a moment she said:

"Pythia! Why should not Pythia marry the King? The Queen does not know she is here and she has never seen me!"

There was silence while both Marcos Roca and the Princess stared first at Erina, then at Pythia.

As the colour came and went in Pythia's cheeks, Erina drew herself from Marcos Roca's arms.

Then she went down on her knees beside Pythia.

"Please . . . Pythia . . . please . . . darling," she begged, "let me marry Marcos! Anyway . . . you understand the Balkans and would be a far better Queen than I could . . . ever be!"

It seemed as if the whole room were waiting for Pythia's answer.

At last in a very small voice she said:

"I will . . . do anything . . . dearest Erina . . . if it . . . will make . . . you happy."

Erina gave a cry, flung her arms round her cousin, and kissed her.

"Oh, Pythia, Pythia," she said, "I know I am asking a great deal! But you are . . . not in love . . . as I am . . . and how can either of us . . . let Mama be in . . . disgrace . . . and have to . . . face the . . . fury of . . . the Queen?"

"I . . . I am sure . . . she will . . . find out," Princess Aileen said in a frightened voice.

"I see no reason why she should," Marcos Roca replied. "Erina has told me when we have talked together that she has never seen the Queen and has never visited the Castle."

"That . . . that is true," the Princess whispered.

"I am just thinking things out," Marcos Roca went on, "and what I suggest, Your Highness, is that Erina and I leave very early tomorrow morning for my own country."

Erina, who still had her arms round Pythia, asked:

"Can we . . . possibly do . . . that?"

"My yacht," Marcos Roca said, "is anchored in

the Thames, and as soon as we have put to sea, my Captain can marry us, which, as you are aware, is perfectly legal."

Erina looked at her mother.

"I have heard that is . . . possible," the Princess said faintly, "but . . . it is a strange way for my daughter to be married!"

"I am aware of that," Marcos said, "but 'needs must when the Devil drives'!"

He spoke lightly.

Then, as if he realised it might be interpreted as an insult directed at the Queen, he said:

"All that matters, Your Highness, is that Erina should be married to me and not to King Alexius."

"B-but . . . suppose . . . they find out?" the Princess asked.

"There is no reason why anybody should suspect such a thing has happened," Erina said. "You know, Mama, nobody at the Castle has taken the slightest interest in us the whole time we have been here. Why should they know that Pythia is here? And if she pretends to be me, why should anybody question her?"

"I believe the British Ambassador to Vultarnia will be calling on me tomorrow," the Princess said, "and Her Majesty intimated to me that if I were not well enough to undertake the journey, the Ambassadress would escort Erina to Vultarnias."

She paused a moment before continuing:

"She will travel in one of the British Battle ships as far as Montenegro."

"If the Ambassador is coming here," Marcos Roca said, "it is essential that Erina and I should

43

leave very early, before he is likely to arrive."

"I am afraid I have no trousseau . . . " Erina began.

"That is another thing," the Princess interrupted. "Her Majesty said that as I had no money, she would give Erina her trousseau, but it would have to be completed before she left in two weeks time."

Erina gave a little laugh.

"If Pythia is not to go to the King barefoot and naked, what about me?"

"You shall have the most beautiful clothes that any bride ever possessed," Marcos Roca promised. "If I consider it safe, we will go first to Paris before we cross the Atlantic to Peru. If not, my darling, you may have to wait for a little while."

"I will go anywhere and wait for years if you tell me to, as long as you are quite . . . certain I can be . . . your wife," Erina said in a low voice.

"I am quite, quite certain, and nothing shall stop us from being married at the latest by tomorrow afternoon," Marcos replied.

The Princess put her hands up to her head.

"You are going too fast and I am frightened . . . terribly frightened at what you are asking me to agree to."

Pythia moved to sit down on the sofa beside her.

"Do not be frightened, Aunt Aileen," she said. "I am your niece and I am sure because you loved Mama and know how happy she was, it will not be difficult to pretend that I am your daughter."

"But . . . the wedding will . . . not be . . . legal," the Princess said frantically, "if you use a false name!"

Pythia smiled.

"You have forgotten, Aunt Aileen, that I too was christened 'Erina.' "

The Princess started.

"Of course!" she said. "I had forgotten! It was my mother's name, and on my wedding day she said to me and to Clodagh:

" 'Because I want you both to be as happy as I have been with your father, and also because I love Ireland, if either of you have a daughter I want you to call her after me.' "

"So you see," Pythia said, "I was christened 'Erina' to please Grandmama, and 'Pythia' because my father was certain I belong to Apollo."

The Princess gave a little sigh.

The girls were not certain whether it was of relief or because she was still desperately worried.

It was then that Marcos Roca took charge of everything.

"You are not to worry," he said. "What I am going to do is leave now and make arrangements to bring a carriage here at seven o'clock tomorrow morning."

He smiled before he went on:

"Erina must be ready to come with me in it to my yacht. No-one will have any idea she had gone, and when the Ambassador calls on the Queen's instructions, all you have to do is to present Miss Pythia as your daughter."

Pythia smiled.

"It all sounds very easy, but I do not want, when I go, to leave Aunt Aileen here alone and terrified that one of us will be exposed."

45

"I have already thought of that," Marcos Roca answered. "I was just going to suggest to the Princess that as soon as you have left for Vultarnia, I will arrange for her to come to Peru. I know my father and my family will welcome her, and she will be provided with a house on our estate."

He smiled at the Princess before he said:

"I am sure, Your Highness, you will make a great many friends who will be very proud to know you, and will certainly not ignore you year after year, as Queen Victoria has done."

"C-can I . . . really do . . . that?" Princess Aileen asked.

"I am not going to allow you to say no," Marcos Roca replied. "I will arrange everything and you will travel on the most comfortable ship available, with a lady's-maid to look after you and a Courier to attend to all your needs during the journey."

Erina gave a cry of delight and once again threw herself into his arms.

"Oh, Marcos, Marcos," she cried, "how can you be so marvellous and make us all so happy! Of course Mama must come to Peru! She has been so lonely and so miserable here without Papa."

"Leave everything to me," Marcos Roca said, "and, of course, Your Highness, it would be a great mistake to tell anyone here where you are going."

He paused and then continued:

"Only some time after you have left England would it be wise to notify Her Majesty that you will not be returning."

"I understand," the Princess said, "and I am

very grateful . . . although I am still afraid that something may go wrong."

"Nothing will go wrong for us," Erina said. "But the person I am worried for is Pythia, who has to marry some frightening man she has never seen."

"I shall be happy just to be in the Balkans again," Pythia answered. "I have not, in fact, visited Vultarnia, but I am sure its language will not be difficult. I shall learn about it from the Ambassador while we are at sea."

"Then that is settled!" Marcos Roca said.

He spoke like a man who was used to solving difficult problems and, of course, having his own way.

He stepped forward to raise the Princess's hand to his lips before he said:

"I thank Your Highness from the bottom of my heart for allowing me to marry your beautiful and adorable daughter. I swear to you on everything I hold sacred that I will make her happy."

The way he spoke was very moving.

Then as he went from the room Erina went with him.

She obviously wished to say farewell in the hall.

Pythia took the Princess's hands in both of hers.

"Do not be upset, Aunt Aileen," she begged, "Erina is very happy, and I think Don Marcos Roca is a charming man."

"I am so frightened," the Princess said. "If the Queen discovers we have deceived her, I cannot think what she will do."

"She will never find out," Pythia said. "I will make certain of that, and in two weeks time we shall all have left England. So why should the Queen be curious about us?"

She saw that her aunt was looking a little happier.

Then, as if she felt it was something she should say, the Princess murmured:

"Are you quite certain, dearest child, you will not be frightened of going to a strange country and marrying a King?"

"Of course it is frightening, put like that," Pythia replied, "but when Erina asked me to help her, I knew that Papa was telling me that was what I must do."

She took a deep breath and then went on:

"I could almost hear his voice. I believe that this was what was planned for me when I was born, and there is no way of avoiding Fate."

She spoke in a dreamy voice, almost as if the words were coming to her mind from another Planet.

For a moment the Princess did not speak. Then she said:

"I am sure, my dear, since you feel like that, that God and Apollo will bless you."

chapter three

MARCOS Roca arrived soon after seven o'clock with a carriage drawn by four horses.

He looked so happy, and so did Erina, that the Princess knew she was doing the right thing in letting them be together.

Before they left, Marcos Roca said to her:

"I have been thinking it over during the night, Ma'am, and I will make certain there will be no possibility of our being discovered before Pythia is married to the King."

The Princess was listening attentively as he went on:

"I have changed my mind about taking Erina to Paris. We will spend our honeymoon on the yacht in the Mediterranean."

He paused for a moment and then went on:

"I will buy part of her trousseau in Marseilles

and Nice, where the Dressmakers can order gowns from Paris to follow us when we arrive home."

The Princess smiled and Marcos Roca went on:

"I feel it would be a mistake, even after we have reached Peru, for Erina to be known by her title and her present name. 'Princess Erina' is so unusual, the British Embassy in Peru, if nobody else, might think it too much of a coincidence."

The Princess realised she had not thought of that.

"I understand," Marcos Roca went on, "she was also christened Moyra, which also is an Irish name. I feel sure that her grandmother, who asked that both Pythia and Erina should be called 'Erina,' would, if she were alive, understand."

"I am sure she would," the Princess agreed, "and I think it very wise of you to take every possible precaution."

"There is no reason why anyone should question the Princess being called 'Moyra,' " Marcos Roca said, "and even if they do, once Pythia is Queen of Vultarnia, there is nothing they can do about it."

"You are right," the Princess told him.

He handed her an envelope.

She found later it contained a large amount of money. It would provide her with everything she needed until she reached Peru.

"Everything will be arranged, Your Highness," he said, "and Erina and I will make you happy and certainly less lonely than you have been these last few years since the death of your husband."

Tears came into Princess Aileen's eyes as she said:

"You are so kind, Marcos, and that Erina should be happy is the answer to all my prayers."

When they left, Marcos, as he was her son-in-law to be, kissed the Princess goodbye, and Erina hugged her mother.

"I can never thank you enough, Mama," she said, "for being so understanding. I am so incredibly lucky to have found Marcos, and it will be wonderful to have you with us when we reach Peru."

They drove off.

The Princess watched them out of sight, the tears running down her cheeks, but they were tears of happiness.

She and Pythia were not alone for long in the thatched cottage before a carriage came to the door.

There was a coachman and a footman on the box, and the latter handed the Princess a note.

It was from the Queen.

When Princess Aileen read it, she gave an exclamation of delight and astonishment.

"What is it?" Pythia asked.

"You will hardly believe it," the Princess replied, "but Her Majesty says that she thought during the night that as we have to buy your trousseau so quickly, we will need a carriage to carry us to London, and it is therefore at our disposal whenever we need it until your marriage!"

"That is certainly very helpful," Pythia said.

She knew it would be very difficult for her aunt to travel any other way.

She did not know about the gift of money from Marcos Roca to the Princess, and she had been wondering frantically how they could afford to hire a carriage.

It just passed through Princess Aileen's mind that the Queen was making reparation for the years of neglect.

Then she thought she was being uncharitable and merely said:

"I am so very, very grateful, and, Pythia darling, we must make you look really beautiful as the Queen of Vultarnia."

The next few days were so exhausting that Pythia knew it would be a mistake for the Princess to do any more.

She therefore managed to secure the services of a respectable woman. She had, until she retired, been a housemaid at Windsor Castle.

She accompanied Pythia to London.

She watched her try on gown after gown and fit those the Princess had already chosen for her.

The Dressmakers, when they learned she was to marry a King, fell over themselves to provide everything that would enhance her beauty.

They were determined she would be the best-dressed woman in Vultarnia.

Because Queen Victoria was paying the bills, Pythia knew there was no need to haggle over the price.

She was able to buy all the things that she and her mother had always longed to own but could never afford.

"I would love to see you dressed in a magnificent white gown, my dearest," her mother had said once, "being presented at Buckingham Palace either to the Queen or else to the very lovely Princess Alexandra."

As they were staying in a rough Inn in the depths of Romania at the time, Pythia had laughed.

"That is as likely, Mama," she said, "as if we thought of flying to the moon or crossing the sea on the back of a dolphin, as Apollo did."

Patrick O'Connor had been vaguely listening to the conversation. He raised his head from the map he was studying.

"As Pythia is dedicated to Apollo," he said, "he will dress her in the gold of the sun and the silver of the moon. What woman could ask for more?"

Pythia thought now it was perhaps Apollo who was responsible for her exquisite trousseau.

Never had she imagined she would ever own silken garments to wear next to her skin.

She had gowns which swept back in the front like the Greek goddesses, and had only a small bustle at the back.

Because, like her mother, she had excellent taste—or perhaps again it was Apollo guiding her—she was very careful to choose nothing that was overpowering.

She bought only gowns that made her look slim and ethereal.

Her taste was instinctive. The same applied to the unique way in which she arranged her hair.

* * *

The British Ambassador to Vultarnia called on the Princess.

When she explained that she was not well enough to travel with her daughter, he promised that he and his wife would look after her very carefully.

"His Majesty has sent a Lady's-maid and an *Aide-de-Camp* on a ship which arrives here to-morrow," he said, "so I assure you the Princess will travel in comfort, and we will try to make up for her not having Your Highness to support her."

It was Pythia who had been very firm in insisting that Princess Aileen should not travel to Vultarnia even for her wedding.

"Surely, dearest," the Princess objected, "I should come with you first before I go to Peru as Marcos had arranged?"

Pythia shook her head.

"We have to disembark at a Port which is the farthest South on the coast of Montenegro and cross the mountains of Albania to reach Vultarnia," she explained. "It is a journey which would be far too exhausting for you to undertake."

The Princess protested, but at the same time she was very relieved.

Her arthritis gave her much pain.

She had no wish, if Pythia was right, to be bumped for miles over rough and precipitous roads.

She therefore made arrangements with the Courier who had been sent to her by Marcos Roca.

He promised to reserve for her accommodation on the first suitable ship sailing to Peru after Pythia had started her journey to Vultarnia.

"You will be very comfortable in a large ship,"

Pythia told her. "Mama and I always wished we could enjoy such comfort instead of putting up with cargo boats which were often very uncomfortable and smelly!"

She gave a little laugh.

At the same time, she was remembering how happy they had been.

They had laughed at the discomfort and even joked about the food that was almost inedible.

"That is what love means," she told herself. "Being happy and content regardless of material discomfort."

From the moment she said goodbye to Princess Aileen and started on her journey to Vultarnia she certainly did not experience that.

The Battle ship in which she was to travel was one of the latest iron-clad vessels.

It was, in fact, going on duty in the Mediterranean, where it was to join five other British Battle ships

The Ambassador was aware why they were sailing to the Eastern Mediterranean.

It was to give a show of strength should the rumours circulating about Russia's intention be substantiated.

As a future Queen, Pythia was given the Captain's cabin, which was large and very comfortable.

The Ambassador and his wife were next door and her maid not far away.

Also to attend her was the *Aide-de-Camp* to the King, whose name was Major Njego Danilo.

He was a tall, good-looking man who looked exceedingly smart in his uniform.

He was formal and somewhat stiff until Pythia informed him that she wished to learn his language.

After his first look of surprise there was, she thought, a mocking expression in his eyes.

She guessed he thought it unlikely that she would be capable of even a few words before they reached their destination.

"The Major is giving me a two-hour lesson in his language every morning," Pythia told the Ambassador.

He replied approvingly:

"That is very sensible of you, although I am afraid you will find it a difficult language. Of course, His Majesty speaks French, Italian, and English."

"That is not surprising," the Ambassadress remarked somewhat tartly, "considering the time he spent roaming all over Europe before he came to the throne."

Pythia was aware of the warning glance the Ambassador gave his wife.

The Ambassadress went on somewhat lamely:

"So many people are proficient in different languages these days!"

The first morning after they had left England the sea was calm and the sun was shining.

Immediately after breakfast Pythia was waiting in the Captain's cabin for Major Danilo.

He came in and bowed to her and to the Ambassadress.

He put some books and a writing-pad down on the table.

"If I had known Your Highness wished to learn

my language," he said to Pythia, "I would have equipped myself more efficiently before I left Vultarnia. All I have with me are some books I brought to read myself, which I am afraid you will find quite incomprehensible."

Pythia smiled, but she did not contradict him.

After she had seated herself at the table, the Ambassadress left them and went to her own cabin.

They were alone.

She felt that Major Danilo was trying to think how he could best start with someone who did not know a single word of Vultarnian.

"I think your language," she said quietly, "like those of most of the Balkan States, is a mixture of Greek, Macedonian, and Asian."

She paused a moment and then went on:

"Of course they all vary, but there is a common denominator between them all which makes it easy to switch from one to the other."

Major Danilo looked at her in sheer astonishment.

"Are you telling me, Your Highness, that you know any of these languages?"

Pythia smiled.

"I am, of course, fluent in Greek, and I can make myself understood in Romanian, Serbian, and Montenegran, all of which I suspect will turn up somewhere in Vultarnian!"

The Major stared at her as if he thought she must be exaggerating.

Pythia opened one of the books he had brought with him.

She found she could quickly make sense of what was printed as soon as she could grasp the first few words of the sentence.

By the time the lesson came to an end she knew she would soon understand Vultarnian.

It was, in fact, very like Montenegran and had a great number of Greek words in its vocabulary.

As they finished, Major Danilo closed the book and said:

"I find it hard to believe that I am not dreaming, Your Highness. I was thinking, when I came to your cabin, that I would be fortunate if by the time we arrived in Vultarnia you could say, 'How do you do' and 'Good morning!' "

He smiled and went on:

"Now I know that the people of my country will be deeply touched that you are able to speak their language."

Pythia smiled as she said:

"I assure you, Major Danilo, I intend to work very hard so that I can not only speak Vultarnian but also understand the problems of the people of Vultarnia. I intend to be word-perfect in your language, which is soon to be *my* language!"

She knew as she saw the expression in the Major's eyes that he was both thrilled and delighted with her.

The next day the sea was very rough in the Bay of Biscay.

However, it did not prevent them from working hard to approach Pythia's idea of perfection.

She also plied the Ambassador and his wife with

questions about the country, and inevitably about the King.

"Tell me about him," she begged.

Although they answered, she had the idea, and she knew it was not just her imagination, that they were keeping something from her.

When they reached the Mediterranean the sea was calm.

It was also warm and sunny, so every moment when she was not working with Major Danilo, she went out on deck.

The ship was fascinating, and the seamen looked at her with admiration.

She found herself a secluded spot which was out of the wind.

She was also protected from the sun and could read the Major's books that were written in Vultarnian.

One day, deeply absorbed in what she was reading, she suddenly became aware of voices.

She realised they came through the port-holes of the superstructure against which she was sitting.

There were two men talking, and she knew after a moment that it was the Ambassador and the Major.

"I gather," the Ambassador said, "that Her Highness is already remarkably proficient in your language. That should certainly be a pleasant surprise for His Majesty when she arrives."

"It will indeed," the Major replied, "especially since, as Your Excellency knows, he has a dislike of the English."

The Ambassador sighed.

"I know that the Prime Minister was right in thinking that an English Queen in Vultarnia will be a better defence than anything else could be."

"Certainly more effective than the guns we do not possess," Major Danilo said bitterly.

There was silence.

Then in his own language, as if he were afraid of being overheard, the Major said:

"What really worries me, Your Excellency, is how the Princess, who is so young and so innocent, can possibly cope with a man like the King."

"The same thought worries me," the Ambassador replied.

"When I left a week after your departure," the Major went on, "they were saying at Court that the King had no intention of giving up the Countess Natasha."

What he said obviously startled the Ambassador, for he exclaimed:

"He cannot mean to keep her in the Palace once he is married!"

"I am sure of one thing," the Major replied, "that the Countess will fight like the devil to stay where she is and to keep the King in her clutches!"

The Ambassador did not speak, and he continued:

"If you ask me, she is a Russian spy! She probably sends reports back to St. Petersburg so that if anything occurs in the country, the Russians will make it an excuse to move in."

"That is something I have thought myself," the Ambassador agreed, "but with an English Queen they would not dare!"

"Are you sure of that?" the Major asked.

"I had a long talk with Mr. Disraeli when I was in London," the Ambassador answered, "and I am totally convinced of one thing, that Russia does not wish to fight Britain."

"I only hope you are right," the Major said, "but I hear they are mobilising their forces."

"Mr. Disraeli is aware of that," the Ambassador replied, "and whatever happens in the Balkans, we can only pray that with the Union Jack flying over Vultarnia, that country will be spared."

"That is what I also hope," the Major said. "At the same time, I am very worried about the Princess."

"She is enchanting!" the Ambassador exclaimed. "But you know better than anybody else that His Majesty is completely unpredictable."

"That is true," the Major agreed. "He loathes being driven or forced into anything he does not wish to do."

The Ambassador sighed again.

"If only Her Majesty the Queen could have found someone older and more experienced than the Princess Erina!"

"From my conversation with her," the Major remarked, "I find her surprisingly wise about things which are important. But whether that will appeal to His Majesty is a very different story."

"We can only hope and pray," the Ambassador said. "And I know that you, Major, will keep me informed if I can help in any way should the Princess be desperately unhappy."

"You know I will do that," the Major answered.

Pythia, listening, heard the sound of footsteps.

She realised the two men had left whichever cabin they were in and there was silence.

She sat staring out to sea, thinking over what she had overheard.

She realised as if for the first time that the task ahead of her was not just to understand the people of Vultarnia, but also their King.

She had impulsively agreed to marry him so that her cousin could escape with Marcos Roca.

At that moment she had not thought of the King as a man, but rather as a country.

She had loved being in the Balkans with her father.

She thought to be there again with the smiling, good-humoured people they had known and loved would be all she could ask of life.

She had, in fact, although she had never said so, found it very dull in the thatched cottage at Windsor.

She had often felt as if the walls were closing in on her.

They were a prison from which she could see no escape.

She was used to the great vistas over the valleys or the heights of the snow-clad mountains.

There had always been something new to discover, unexpected problems like fording rivers, or avoiding an avalanche.

There were nights when they had slept under the stars.

At other times they had stayed in some delightful small village, or in a town where they were welcomed and her father was acclaimed for his medical skills.

It had all been, as her mother had said from the very beginning, a great adventure.

At Windsor she was beginning to wonder how she could bear the long days when there was no one new to talk to.

Everything the Princess and Erina said seemed to have been said a dozen times before.

From the moment she made the decision to take her cousin's place, she was sure she would love Vultarnia.

But now there was a very different question, and that was—would she love the King?

She thought this question over and changed it to what was really more important—would the King love her?

It had never struck her that he might be against the idea of marrying an Englishwoman.

She was aware that a great number of men had mistresses.

Yet she had not envisaged the King having one at this particular moment.

She had certainly never dreamed that she would be a Russian.

When she had been with her father and mother in Romania, the people had talked about the menace of the Russians on their Northern border.

In the countries farther South, especially Bulgaria, they had suffered from the ghastly onslaught of the Turks.

They had committed atrocities which her father would not repeat to her.

Knowing the Balkans as she did, she could understand the menace that confronted them now.

It was not the Ottoman Empire as it had been in the past, but the greed and ambition of Russia.

How, in those circumstances, she asked herself, unless he was extremely stupid, could the King have a Russian mistress?

She was well aware that the Russians were suspected of having spies everywhere.

The frightening network of "The Third Section" was whispered about wherever they went.

Her father had talked about it a great deal.

At the same time, it was very easy to kindle fear in simple folk.

They themselves, as foreigners, had often been received coldly and with suspicion.

Then, when people learnt that her father was Irish and more important than anything else a Doctor, doors opened.

His medical skill was a universal "Open Sesame."

They all told him of their aches and pains.

But the older members of each community confided in him also their fears and doubts for their safety and for peace.

"Surely the King must know all this?" Pythia asked herself.

When next she was alone with the Ambassadress she said:

"Do tell me a little more about the King. I have been too shy to ask many questions about him, but naturally I am curious."

"Of course you are, Your Highness," the Ambassadress replied. "I can tell you that he is very handsome and most women find him irresistible."

"But has he not been lonely since he came to the throne?" Pythia asked.

It seemed an innocent question. But she was aware the Ambassadress gave her a somewhat sharp glance before she replied:

"Of course His Majesty has many friends."

"Are they all Vultarnians?"

"Oh, no!" the Ambassadress replied. "As His Majesty has travelled extensively, he has visitors from all the countries of Europe, many of them, as you can imagine, wanting to see how he is faring as a Monarch after a life of pleasure with no responsibilities."

"It must have been a tremendous change for him," Pythia said. "I have heard, but I cannot remember how, that he was in love with someone whom he could not marry."

The Ambassadress stiffened.

Then she said coldly:

"There has been no question of the King marrying anyone until now."

"But he has been in love?" Pythia persisted.

The Ambassadress drew in her breath.

"You are very young, Your Highness," she said. "At the same time, I am sure you must be aware that men are often what one might call 'infatuated' by women who in no circumstances can they marry."

"If that is so," Pythia said, "surely a man would be unhappy at having to give up a woman who meant so much to him because he had to marry somebody else?"

She saw the Ambassadress was thinking desperately of a suitable answer.

Finally she said:

"Of course with his attractions and his position, the King has many women pursuing him, and he would be inhuman if he were not flattered by their attentions."

"And do you think," Pythia said in a small voice, "that His Majesty will be interested in an Englishwoman he has never seen, who has been sent to him simply because she is British and protection for Vultarnia from the Russians?"

"I think, Your Highness," the Ambassadress said briefly, "you must talk to my husband about this. I am afraid I am very foolish about politics, but I know one thing, my dear, and that is that the women of Vultarnia will welcome you with open arms."

Pythia thought for a moment that that was rather cold comfort.

She knew she was, in fact, very nervous of what she would find when she reached Vultarnia.

Supposing, she asked herself, the King took an instant dislike to her?

After what she had heard the Major and the Ambassador saying, that was very likely.

Then, almost as if she could hear him speaking to her, she knew her father was telling her that this was her Fate, her Karma.

It was what he had envisaged when he had offered her up to Apollo after she was born.

There was something, though she was not yet sure what it was, that she had to do for Vultarnia.

She could only pray that when the time came, Apollo would guide her, and she would do what was right.

"Help me, Papa, help me!" she asked that night after she had said her prayers.

She crossed the cabin to a port-hole and looked up at the sky.

The moon was shining amongst the stars.

She thought that the light of it reflected in the sea below was very beautiful.

It was the Light of Apollo, the Light under which she had been born, and which would always guide and protect her.

As she climbed into bed she felt her fears leaving her.

She would live up to her real name. The words which came into her mouth as Pythia would be those of the god who spoke through her.

chapter four

WHEN the Battle ship moved into the Port of Cattaro, Pythia could see the mountains of Albania in the distance.

She felt that she had come home.

The sight that most moved her heart was the smiling faces of the Montenegrans.

She had learnt when she was last there of their age-old struggle for independence against the Turks.

The long fight for liberation had developed in them, her father had thought, the manly virtues of heroism and endurance.

"They are," Patrick O'Connor said, "an inspiration to all the countries near them in the way they have endured personal sacrifice and never lost their determination to reach their goal."

There was a crowd to see Pythia, with the Ambassador and his wife, followed by Major Danilo, as they came down the gangway.

Waiting for them were carriages to carry them on the arduous journey to Vultarnia.

One carriage was filled with the luggage.

Another conveyed the Ambassador's Valet, his wife's Lady's-maid, and, of course, Aphaia, which was the name of the woman who had been sent to look after Pythia.

In order to practise the Vultarnian language with her, they talked all the time she was dressing and undressing.

Just before they reached the port, she said to Aphaia:

"Are your people pleased with their King?"

There was a little pause before the maid replied:

"He has been on the throne only a year, Your. Highness."

"A year is long enough to know whether one likes a person or not," Pythia replied with a smile.

Aphaia looked over her shoulder as if afraid she might be overheard before she said:

"His Majesty is very European, Your Highness, and my people are simple and do not understand the ways of the world outside our own country."

"What you are saying," Pythia remarked, "if you are truthful, is that Vultarnia is slightly backward."

Aphaia nodded:

"That is true, Your Highness. I have seen several other countries when I travelled with Her Majesty and also with some of His late Majesty's relatives."

"So you think that something needs to be

changed in Vultarnia," Pythia said beneath her breath.

She was perceptively aware that Aphaia was wondering whether she dared say what was in her mind.

Impulsively Pythia said:

"Please be honest with me. I know I have a great deal to learn, and it would be very helpful if you would be kind enough to be frank and outspoken instead of leaving me to find out everything for myself."

She knew the way she spoke had touched the maid's heart.

Coming a little nearer to her, the maid said in a low voice:

"There are young people in the City who say that we must move with the times. We thought that His Majesty, when he succeeded, would introduce a great many innovations and up-to-date ideas to make us prosperous."

"But he has not done that!" Pythia said.

Aphaia sighed.

"Men, Your Highness, are the same all the world over: when they are young and handsome they seek amusement."

There was a little hesitation before the maid added beneath her breath:

" . . . and a pretty woman to share it with."

Pythia had found out what she wanted to know: that Vultarnia was out of date.

She knew that Montenegro was trying to build new towns and new industries now that they had their freedom.

She would have liked to visit the capital, Cetinje, again and see what was being done there.

Among the carriages waiting for them there was one for the high-ranking Officers who had come to escort them to Vultarnia.

The Officers bowed respectfully to Pythia, but discussed everything that had been arranged with the Ambassador.

Pythia was sure that in their eyes she was just a young and ignorant Englishwoman.

She would have no idea of the difficulties of travelling to Vultarnia.

Anyway, she would not understand them if they spoke to her.

She therefore allowed herself to be helped to the largest and most impressive of the carriages.

It was drawn by what she thought were the finest horses.

She was to drive with the Ambassadress and Major Danilo.

The Ambassador was invited to drive with the Officers.

Behind them came the servants and the luggage.

There was a Brake for the soldiers which they occupied while they drove along good level roads in Montenegro.

When they reached the mountains of Albania, they marched on either side of the carriage.

Pythia was aware that they could have avoided the climb if they had gone farther into Montenegro.

They could then have circled round the most Northerly point of Albania, where it peaked into that country.

It would, in fact, not have taken very much longer.

There was, however, a road rough but negotiable which could take them straight over the mountains and down into Vultarnia.

The climb up strained the horses' endurance to the limit.

Pythia was thankful that the Princess Aileen was not with them.

She would certainly have suffered if she had been thrown from side to side, as they were.

Even though the carriage was thickly padded, Pythia felt as if her whole body would be bruised by the time they reached the summit.

The soldiers escorting them on foot stumbled over huge stones or sank ankle-deep in muddy puddles.

They had stopped for a picnic luncheon which Pythia enjoyed.

The Ambassadress, on the other hand, said she felt sick.

All she wanted was to arrive as soon as possible at their destination.

"I know, my dear, how uncomfortable it is," her husband said sympathetically. "At the same time, if we had gone the whole way round, in Montenegran territory, they would have felt obliged, because Princess Erina was with us, to welcome her."

He smiled before he said:

"We would have had to listen to a great many speeches and certainly to partake of a very heavy luncheon before we could have been on our way!"

"On the whole," the Ambassadress replied, "I think I prefer being buffeted about as if I were a pea out of a pod!"

Her husband persuaded her to drink a little brandy.

She also sipped the excellent wine which was provided with the luncheon.

After that she felt better.

It was a relief to know that the Monastery where they were to stay the night was now less than two miles away.

They were, however, all very tired when they reached the Monastery.

It was an ancient building in which over fifty monks lived.

They worshipped with their Abbot in a very beautiful Chapel which they had built and decorated themselves.

They also catered for a great number of travellers every year and saved them from being robbed or terrorised by brigands.

The rooms which Pythia and her party were to occupy for the night in the Guest-House were plain but spotlessly clean.

The beds were not as uncomfortable as the Ambassadress had feared.

"I am quite prepared," she said, "to repent of my sins, but not on a hard board after my body feels as if it had been rocked on a bed of sharp stones."

Pythia laughed, but she did, in fact, feel very sympathetic.

They ate by themselves on an ancient refectory table in the Sitting-Room of the Guest-House.

Afterwards they were received by the Abbot.

He was a very impressive-looking man and had a spiritual aura about him that Pythia sensed immediately.

She thought he looked at her in a penetrating manner.

After they had talked for some time, the Ambassadress said she would like to retire to bed.

"I think we should all have a good night's sleep," the Ambassador said. "It will be quite a long journey before we reach Vultarnia, and when we do arrive, the Cabinet will be waiting to welcome Her Highness into the country before we reach the Palace."

"It sounds exhausting," the Ambassadress complained, "and I am quite sure it will be!"

Pythia had also risen to her feet.

When she would have left with the rest of the party, the Abbot said:

"I would like a private word with Your Highness, if you will be kind enough to listen to me."

"But of course," Pythia answered.

They were speaking in English, but the Abbot was far from fluent and he stumbled over a number of words.

Therefore, when they were alone, Pythia said:

"I speak Vultarnian, Holy Father."

He looked at her in surprise before he said in that language:

"That will be a great blessing in the work that lies ahead of you."

Pythia looked up at him.

"You know there is something important for me to do in Vultarnia?"

He nodded, and she was aware that he was wondering how he could put into words what was expected of her.

Very quietly she said:

"I am aware, Holy Father, that what I have to do does not rest on the fact that I am British, but I am not certain yet what it is."

She smiled at him before continuing:

"However, I know it is God's will that I should come to Vultarnia."

The Abbot's face lit up.

"That is what I wanted you to feel, my child. There are, in fact, many things that must be done in Vultarnia if its people are to be saved, and not only from any external menace."

"I promise you," Pythia said, "that I will do anything that is within my power. But I need, Holy Father, your prayers and, if it is possible, your guidance."

"I will pray," the Abbot said, "that you will be guided, and I think already you are aware from where that guidance will come."

Pythia nodded and he said:

"If there is anything I can do at any time, you can call on me either spiritually or as an ordinary human being. Do you understand?"

"I understand, Holy Father," Pythia replied, "and I am very grateful."

Without being told, she knelt down in front of the Abbot.

He blessed her and she felt as he did so as if a light were blazing above her head.

Although her eyes were shut, she could both feel and see it.

It was the Divine Light of Apollo which came from God and with the sunrise brought Light to the Earth and swept away the darkness.

It was in the moonlight which promised that the day would come again when Apollo drove across the sky.

When the Abbot finished his Blessing, Pythia rose and he smiled at her as if she had made him happy.

"I shall not see Your Highness in the morning," he said, "but go in peace, and know that God is with you."

Pythia genuflected.

When she opened the door of the room she found Major Danilo waiting to take her safely to her bedroom.

They walked in silence until they stopped at her door. Then she said:

"The Abbot is a very holy man."

"We know in Vultarnia that he watches over us as well as over those in Montenegro."

"I am glad, very glad that he is here," Pythia remarked, "and now that he has blessed me I am not as frightened as I was about meeting the King."

For a moment the Major said nothing.

Then, unexpectedly, he went down on one knee and kissed her hand.

"Whatever happens in the future," he said quietly, "I dedicate myself to Your Highness's service, and if you call on me for help, I swear I will never fail you!"

Pythia was very touched.

Then as he rose she said:

"Thank you . . . thank you, for all you have . . . done for me . . . already!"

She did not wait for his answer, but went into her bedroom and shut the door.

As she stood at the window, looking up at the stars, she told herself that she was very fortunate.

Whatever difficulties there might be ahead, she knew she would at least be doing something worthwhile, not just vegetating in an isolated cottage in Windsor Park.

"It is a great adventure!" she told the stars.

She thought she heard her father laugh, because that was what he had expected life to hold for her.

*   *   *

The next morning the party started early.

At first it was nearly as bumpy going downhill as it had been coming up.

The difference was that it was a great deal faster.

They soon reached a track that zig-zagged through the fir trees.

It was noon when they stopped for luncheon.

Now Pythia could see a long way below the country over which she was to reign.

Even in the distance it looked very beautiful.

Later, when they drew nearer, she found it enchanting.

The mountains of Vultarnia were linked with those of Albania.

Beneath them were cascades, rivers, and lakes.

There were long vistas merging into the misty horizon which made the beauty of it seem as if it were part of a dream.

Although the sun was shining, it was not too hot.

When Pythia asked if it was possible to have the carriage open, the hood was let down at the back.

Now she could see better than she had before.

She realised, as she had half-expected, that Vultarnia was much less cultivated than Montenegro.

There were great stretches of land that were completely uninhabited.

The valleys were brilliant with the wild flowers which grew amid the long grass.

In other Balkan countries, where there was a river winding through the land, it would have been cultivated.

The peasants wearing their National Costume would be working there from dawn until dusk.

They passed through some small villages, the houses of which looked neglected.

The children waved as they drove by and were obviously delighted with the soldiers.

But Pythia thought they looked thin, and were not as rosy-cheeked as they should be.

She did not, however, comment on what she thought.

She was aware that Major Danilo was watching her.

The Ambassadress, who had not slept well, dozed in her corner on the back seat.

Finally, at four o'clock in the afternoon, they reached the outskirts of the Capital.

Pythia could see in the distance that it was surrounded by an ancient wall.

When they neared the great gateway she could see a huge crowd of people waiting to greet her.

Major Danilo noticed that she looked a little apprehensive, and he bent forward to say:

"If you thank them in their own language, they will be delighted!"

Pythia smiled at him.

"I have just been turning it over in my mind."

"You will be sensational!" he said reassuringly.

The carriage came to a standstill and the door was opened by a soldier.

They had stopped exactly opposite a platform on which there stood a dozen important-looking men.

They were all somewhat elderly, and she guessed that one of them was the Prime Minister.

The crowd which was clustered around the platform was staring at her.

They were silent as she walked from the carriage up the steps and onto the platform.

As Pythia shook hands with the Prime Minister, those nearest began to clap.

"Welcome, Your Highness, to our country!" the Prime Minister said in broken English. "It is a very great honour to have you here, and everyone in Vultarnia will do their best to make you happy."

He did not wait for Pythia to reply.

He introduced to her one after the other those on the platform, who she realised were the Members of the Cabinet.

Only when the introductions had been made did the Prime Minister say to the Ambassador:

"There will be no speeches here because His Majesty is waiting at the Palace for Her Highness and it is important she should not be late."

"I understand," the Ambassador said.

The Prime Minister obviously expected this information to be transmitted to Pythia, as he had spoken in his own language.

The Ambassador looked at her.

She moved to stand beside the Prime Minister instead of facing him.

Now the crowd clustered round the platform could see her clearly, and she said in a strong, clear voice in Vultarnian:

"I want to thank you, Prime Minister, and everyone here for your welcome. I am sure when I know Vultarnia as well as you do, I shall love such a beautiful, warm-hearted country!"

There was a little gasp as she finished speaking.

Then the crowd began to cheer.

As they did so, the Prime Minister said:

"It is very kind and clever of Your Highness to speak to us in our own language."

"I have had a good teacher in Major Danilo," Pythia answered.

She knew the Prime Minister and the other people present assumed that she had just learnt the speech.

She had, in fact, made it parrot-fashion.

She thought it would be a mistake to reveal now that she could speak Vultarnian fluently.

Instead, she said goodbye, shaking hands with all the Cabinet.

She was assisted into the carriage.

Now the Ambassador sat beside her while his wife sat on the seat opposite with Major Danilo.

As they drove through the gates and into the City there were a small number of Union Jacks.

They fluttered beside the flag of Vultarnia, which was coloured orange, white, and green.

The roads of the City were lined with people.

Once again Pythia was aware that they were not as well dressed as in the Capitals of other Balkan countries.

She could see that many of the houses needed paint and repairs.

The Churches required cleaning, and there were broken windows in the Cathedral.

"Is the whole country very poor?" she asked the Ambassador.

"One gets an impression of poverty," the Ambassador replied, "though a great number of the aristocratic landlords are rich. However, here in the City there are no new industries, which means that unfortunately a great number of men are unemployed."

"I suppose I should have asked before what are the natural resources in Vultarnia," Pythia said. "Have they any minerals?"

"Quite a number," the Ambassador replied. "But they have not been mined and, as you have seen as we drove along, a great deal of the land is not cultivated."

As they were speaking, Pythia was waving to the crowds.

They waved back, not particularly enthusiastically, but at least she was something new.

The procession with escort of the soldiers who had been joined by other Troops at the City gates was colourful.

Suddenly ahead of her Pythia saw the Palace.

The sun was shining on it where it stood high above the City.

It was white and looked like a jewel surrounded by a profusion of green trees.

The Royal Standard was flying in the breeze.

They drew nearer, and the horses began to climb up the hill on which it was built.

Now Pythia could see there were two fountains playing in front of the Palace.

The gardens in which they stood were brilliant with flowers.

There was hibiscus everywhere, and climbing geraniums covered the walls of the terraces.

There was a long flight of steps at the bottom of which the horses stopped.

Pythia felt a constriction of her heart.

Now for the first time she would see the man she was to marry.

* * *

The King said somewhat reluctantly as the afternoon wore on:

"I suppose I should go and put on my finery to meet this damned woman!"

He spoke in French.

The Countess Natasha rose from the couch on which she had been reclining.

She was wearing a diaphanous negligée which revealed rather than concealed her figure.

Round her neck was a necklace of emeralds which the King had just given her.

"*Mon pauvre!*" she replied. "I know how agonising this is for you, but I will be near you and as long as we can be together, as we are now, why should some fat, dull Englishwoman be of any consequence?"

"I have no wish to marry!" the King said petulantly.

"I know that," the Countess murmured, "and all this talk by your Prime Minister is merely to frighten you into giving them a Queen who they think will listen to their endless complaints."

"Do you think your country is really likely to invade us?" the King asked.

The Countess laughed, and it was like the sound of tinkling bells.

"No, of course not! Why should Russia, which is already so large, wish to gain more land? Your Statesmen have just made her a 'Bogey-Bogey' with which to frighten a little boy!"

As she spoke she put her arms around the King's neck, and her lips were on his.

He held her against him, feeling the warmth and softness of her body.

But as her lips became more passionate he pushed her to one side.

"You are not to tempt me, Natasha!" he protested. "Anyway, you have already tired me out!"

"I do not believe that," the Countess answered. "There has never been a man as strong and ardent as you! Ah, *Mon cher*, why must you leave me?"

She would have embraced him again, but he walked towards the door.

As he reached it she gave a little cry.

"When shall I see you again?"

The King's eyes twinkled.

"I imagine it will be only a few hours before I find the Union Jack insufferable."

The Countess laughed.

Then, as she flung out her arms as if she were inviting him to take possession of her, he went from the room.

He walked from the Guest Wing of the Palace into the main building, which was quite a considerable way.

He passed flunkeys on duty and several Gentlemen-in-Waiting and *Aides-de-Camp* who were moving about their business.

He had no idea of the knowing look in their eyes as they were aware of where he had been.

There was a somewhat mocking twist to their lips.

Everybody in the Palace talked about the King's infatuation with the Russian Countess.

They had to admit, however, that although the

association was unfortunate, it was understandable.

There was not a man in the whole Palace who was not aware that the Princess Natasha Zarlinski was the embodiment of sensual exoticism.

Every word she spoke, every movement she made, was designed to attract any man who was near her.

She was beautiful in a very Russian manner.

She had dark hair which had blue lights in it, and green eyes which slanted up a little at the sides.

She had a dazzling white skin which rivalled the snow on the peaks of the mountains.

They could all understand the King's obsession.

At the same time, Vultarnia was being neglected, and the whole country was aware of it.

He certainly looked a King as he strolled down the corridors.

His handsome face and square shoulders were reflected in the gilt-framed mirrors which hung on the walls.

When eventually he reached his own apartments his Valet was waiting for him.

Hanging over the back of a chair was his white tunic with its medals and decorations in which he was to receive the future Queen of Vultarnia.

He did not speak for a moment but merely pulled off his shirt and started to wash.

He was aware as he did so that he could smell on his skin the exotic perfume which Natasha always used.

It came from France.

He had sent for several bottles of it only the other week, thinking that it was absurdly expensive.

It had, of course, cost nothing like the amount he had spent on the emerald necklace.

He felt he had to give her something.

She had wept bitterly at the news that he was to be married at the request of his Prime Minister and the Foreign Secretary.

"What else can I do but agree?" he asked.

"It is only because they want to get rid of me!" Natasha sobbed. "If I have to leave you, my wonderful, splendid lover, I swear I shall—die!"

"Do you really think I can let you leave me?" the King had asked.

He took her into his arms.

The fire within them both leapt wildly into the sky, and there was no longer any need for words.

He thought now how beautiful she was, and irresistibly attractive.

He had called on her after luncheon.

He wanted to talk to her before he prepared himself to meet his English bride and to face the boredom of having dinner with her.

Natasha had been waiting for him.

As he came into the room he saw she was naked.

Only the emerald necklace he had given her the night before gleamed against her white skin.

It was a night in which he had been unable to sleep until the dawn had broken, when he was no longer capable of feeling the fire that had consumed him.

Yet there had been no need for words.

She had melted into his arms.

Only now with a tremendous effort had he been able to leave her.

He was buttoning his shirt when there was a knock on the door.

The Valet opened it and an *Aide-de-Camp* resplendent in full dress uniform saluted the King.

"I beg to inform Your Majesty that the carriage bringing Her Highness Princess Erina is within sight."

"They must be early!" the King exclaimed.

"Actually, Your Majesty, they are late, but I expect the road over the mountains is as bad as it was two months ago."

The King remembered the road very well.

He had become extremely impatient at the slow progress made by his horses.

He wanted to reach the Palace, where Natasha was waiting for him.

Never in a long line of mistresses all over Europe had he known anyone so alluring, or so insatiable.

"I am damned if I will give her up!" he told himself beneath his breath.

Then as he realised that the *Aide-de-Camp* was looking anxious at the delay, he put on his white tunic.

His Valet draped over his shoulder the ribbon of the Cross of St. Vitus.

"I am ready!" he said curtly.

He knew as he spoke that the *Aide-de-Camp* was thinking:

'And not before time!'

But the man only bowed politely.

The King walked ahead along the broad corridors which led to the front of the Palace.

He went down the stairs.

He could see through a window that the carriage containing the Englishwoman was already drawn up at the foot of the steps.

He deliberately refused to hurry himself.

He could feel his fury rising within him.

Just to calm the fears of a few stupid old Statesmen, he had to marry a woman he had never seen before and would certainly dislike on sight.

The hall was filled with Officers, Officials, Gentlemen-in-Waiting, and *Aides-de-Camp*.

Their faces were all turned towards him.

Footmen pulled open the glass doors, and still without hurrying himself the King stepped through them.

That damned Englishwoman was already half-way up the steps.

chapter five

THE King was laughing.

As he looked around the room he saw that everybody else was laughing too.

He had expected to sit through dinner, finding the Englishwoman he was forced to marry an unutterable bore.

Instead of which he had been stunned from the moment he saw her.

He had made up his mind, as he had said to Natasha, that she would be large, fat, and plain.

But when Pythia reached the top of the steps he saw she was small, frail, and beautiful in an ethereal way that he had never imagined.

She was exquisitely dressed in a pale *eau-de-nil* gown.

The bodice outlined the curves of her breasts and her tiny waist.

She curtsied to him with a grace which he recognised was unusual.

When she rose, he looked into her blue eyes fringed with dark lashes and felt he must be dreaming.

He had deliberately arranged only a small dinner-party.

He had expected he would be ashamed of the woman who was to be his bride, instead of which he knew that Pythia had captivated everybody from the moment she walked into the room.

She was wearing a white gown which reminded him of something, although he could not think for the moment what it was.

The only colour besides her eyes was a small pink rose in her hair.

She curtsied and smiled at him shyly.

He took her round and introduced her to his relations and several of the Officers who were on duty in the Palace.

He was aware that they were all fascinated by anything so delicate and so very young.

During dinner he said to her:

"Am I really to believe that you are English?"

Her eyes seemed to twinkle at him as she replied:

"My mother and my grandfather would be insulted by such a suggestion!"

For a moment the King did not understand. Then he exclaimed:

"Of course—Irish! I apologise!"

"We are very proud of our emerald isle," Pythia said.

"If all the women on it look like you," the King said, "I cannot imagine why I have not found time to go there!"

Pythia felt sad that while her father talked about and loved her namesake country, she had herself actually never been there.

Patrick O'Connor had in fact been meaning to take his wife and daughter to his home after their visit to Italy.

Then he was drowned and Pythia had spent a dull and empty year in Windsor Park.

"I think," the King said, when they left the Dining-Room and walked towards the Drawing-Room, "that I should congratulate you on your gowns."

He paused and smiled at her before continuing:

"If all your trousseau is as elegant as the two I have seen you wearing so far, I shall be looking forward each day to admiring you."

"For that you must certainly thank the English," Pythia replied, "for my trousseau was a gift from Queen Victoria."

"I had no idea that she had such good taste!" the King exclaimed.

Then they were both laughing again.

Only when a little later the evening was drawing to an end did Pythia ask:

"What has been planned for us for tomorrow?"

"A multitude of extremely boring things," the King answered. "You have to be introduced to the Members of Parliament, to receive a number of Deputations, and be grateful for a collection of wedding presents we could well do without!"

"It sounds exhausting!" Pythia remarked.

She looked up at the King.

Then she asked a little shyly:

"Is there any . . . possibility of my . . . being able . . . to ride?"

The King gave an exclamation and said:

"I have heard of the Irish horses, and of course I hope mine will compare favourably with them."

"Then I may . . . ride?" Pythia persisted.

"Only if you will join me at seven o'clock in the morning."

He thought her whole face lit up with excitement.

"Of course I can do that!"

"Then we will ride for an hour-and-a-half before breakfast," the King said.

When she said good night she added:

"I promise I will not be late."

He watched her walk up the stairs beside the other ladies in the party.

When she had disappeared at the top of them he told himself that he was tired.

He had no intention of visiting Natasha, though she would be expecting him to do so.

He went straight to his own room.

When he was finally in bed he was thinking of Pythia.

"She is very different from what I expected," he murmured before he fell asleep.

* * *

Pythia was used to rising early and was out of bed before her maid called her.

She was, of course, used to dressing herself.

She therefore needed very little help in putting on a smart summer habit she had bought in Bond Street.

It had been extremely expensive.

She had wondered if Queen Victoria would consider it a superfluous addition to her wardrobe.

When she told her aunt what she had bought, Princess Aileen had said:

"Do not worry, dearest. If the Queen is disagreeable about what she had to spend, I am sure I can repay her out of the money Marcos has given me."

Then she added:

"Actually, I think that because Her Majesty neglected Erina and me for so long her conscience is pricking her."

Pythia put on the very smart riding-hat that went with the habit.

It was three minutes to seven when she left her room and hurried down the stairs.

The King was already in the hall.

As she joined him she said a little breathlessly:

"I am not late!"

"You are amazingly punctual," he answered, "an unusual virtue in women."

"It depends what sort of women you are talking about," Pythia answered. "I never dared to be late for my father."

She knew as she spoke that she was thinking of Patrick O'Connor and not Prince Lucian, as the King assumed.

She told herself she must be very careful not to confuse them in her mind.

She must not make the King suspicious that she was not who she pretended to be.

They went out through a door at the back of the Palace.

There she saw the two horses that were waiting for them and gave a cry of delight.

When they were mounted, the King led the way through the Palace gardens.

They went down a winding road which led to a valley outside the Town.

There was some level, uncultivated land, seeming to stretch away into infinity.

Some way behind them came two *Aides-de-Camp*.

They kept their distance.

It was clear to Pythia that the King hated to feel he was being closely guarded all the time.

She made no comment but urged her horse forward.

He did the same.

Then they were galloping wildly over the level ground.

Butterflies hovering over the flowers rose in clouds in front of them.

They also disturbed many birds which swept up into the sky.

It was just, Pythia thought, what she needed.

In the same way she and her father and mother had ridden over the Steppes of Romania.

It was something she had missed miserably at Windsor.

Princess Aileen had only one horse which drew

the pony-carriage in which she went shopping with Erina.

Pythia had been allowed to ride the horse when it was not needed.

It was, however, slow, stubborn, and resentful of the exercise it was forced to take.

Now the horse on which she was mounted carried her as swiftly as the wind.

She felt as if she could fly on it into the sky and over the top of the snow-clad mountain peaks.

They rode a long way before drawing in their horses.

The King looked at Pythia's flushed cheeks and the little fair curls which now escaped from under her riding-hat.

"Does that make you feel better?" he asked perceptively.

"Very, very much better!" Pythia replied.

"I thought you were frightened when you arrived," he remarked. "Was it of me?"

"Everything I heard about you was frightening," Pythia replied truthfully, "and I was also afraid that if I hated you and you hated me, it would be very difficult to live with you here in Vultarnia."

"And now?" the King asked.

"The butterflies are no longer fluttering inside me," she said. "They are flying ahead, showing me the way."

He laughed before he replied:

"Everything you say is so different from what I expected. Just as I had no idea anyone could look like you and not come from Mount Olympus."

He gave a sudden exclamation.

"That is what I thought you looked like last night, but I could not put a name to it. It comes, of course, from your Greek blood."

Because she had no wish to lie any more than she had to, Pythia touched her horse with her heel.

He moved restlessly.

"Where do we go now?" she asked.

"Back, unfortunately," the King said, "but by a different route from which we came."

This meant they now had to ride North.

As they turned, Pythia looked back and saw the two *Aides-de-Camp* a long way behind them.

They galloped a little farther.

Then, when the City could just be seen in the distance, they pulled in their horses until they were walking.

"It is all so beautiful!" Pythia exclaimed. "I would like to spend all today just looking at this wild, untouched land."

"I would like to do the same thing," the King agreed. "I always find anything that is my duty . . . a crashing bore!"

It struck Pythia that he should not feel like that.

Somehow she must make him realise that being a reigning Monarch could be very interesting.

Then she told herself she was being presumptuous.

It was unlikely that whatever she said the King would listen to her.

The City was drawing nearer, and there were a few roughly-built wooden houses beside some rocks.

Suddenly from one of them a little boy came running towards them.

"Help! Help!" he cried in Vultarnian. "Please, help me! My mother's in terrible pain!"

As he spoke, Pythia thought she could hear a woman screaming.

Without hesitating she held out her reins to the King, who was riding close beside her, and said:

"I will go to see what is happening."

"There is no need to do that," the King said sharply, but Pythia was not listening.

She had slipped down from the saddle.

She was running beside the small boy back towards the house from which he had come.

As she went inside she saw a very poorly furnished room with a stove, and an open door led into the bedroom.

Now the scream which came from it was deafening.

She went in and realised that a woman lying on the bed was in the last stages of childbirth.

Pythia had never delivered a baby by herself.

But she had often helped her father, and without even thinking about it she pulled off her jacket and her hat.

She saw there was an apron hanging from a nail on the door and put it on.

To the small boy she said:

"Find me all the towels you have in the house and a blanket. And see if you can boil some water for me on the stove."

She had to speak loudly to make herself heard above the noise the woman on the bed was making.

Then she started to talk to her in the quiet, soothing manner which her father had shown to the mothers when he delivered their children.

Instantly the woman seemed to respond and become quieter.

Pythia discovered that the baby was almost born but could not manage to come completely into the world without help.

She remembered exactly what she had seen her father do.

When the small boy returned with a pile of rags which were at least clean and a blanket, she sent him for a bucket.

Nearly ten minutes later the King entered the house.

He had been forced to wait for the *Aides-de-Camp* to join him before he could hand over the horses.

He could not imagine what his future bride was doing.

He thought it extraordinary of her to disappear and not to return.

He was frowning as he walked through the outer room and into the bedroom.

Pythia was holding a baby in her arms, wrapped in a blanket.

She was just about to hand him to his mother, but as she saw the King standing there, she said:

"A new citizen for Your Majesty, and I feel in the circumstances you will most graciously allow him to be called by your name."

For a moment the King just stared at her.

She was looking very lovely, her cheeks flushed, her hair curling untidily over her head.

She was holding the baby close against her breast.

As she wished to make him interested, she moved a little closer to him, saying:

"I am afraid young Alexius is not particularly handsome at the moment, but I am sure, since he bears your name, he will try to emulate you in every way."

The woman had not understood since Pythia had spoken to the King in English.

He knew she was teasing him.

At the same time, as he realised she had actually delivered the child, he could not for the moment find anything to say.

Pythia took the baby to its mother.

"I expect he will soon be hungry," she said in Vultarnian, "and I am sure you are delighted to have a second son."

"Thank ye, Gracious Lady," the woman said weakly, "but be that really His Majesty th' King a-standing there?"

"It is," Pythia said, "and he gives you his blessing and says that your son is to bear his name."

Now she could only gasp:

"Thank ye, Your Majesty, thank ye! Thank ye!"

"You must thank your future Queen," the King said, finding his voice at last. "She is a very remarkable person!"

The woman was too overawed by his presence to do anything but give a faint smile.

Pythia tucked in the bed-clothes.

She told the boy to empty the pail and went into the kitchen to wash her hands.

The King followed her, picking up her jacket and hat from the chair on which she had left them.

She put them on and said to the small boy who was staring at her:

"Where is your father?"

"He's a-gone t' th' City t' buy food."

"That is good," Pythia said. "Tell him to give your mother something to eat and if possible some milk to drink."

The boy, who was about six years old, appeared to understand.

She glanced at the King.

As if he knew what she was asking without words, he drew from his pocket a silver coin.

He gave it to the boy.

There was a shout of delight as he clutched it tightly in his hand.

"You have been very good and helpful to your mother," Pythia said as she smiled.

The King had walked out of the house and she followed him.

As she reached him she said:

"I was only just in time. If I had not been there, the baby would have died!"

"How did you know what to do?" the King asked, perplexed.

Pythia almost told him the truth before she exclaimed:

"We shall have to hurry! We shall now be late for the first Deputation, and whichever one it is will make us late for all the rest."

An *Aide-de-Camp* who had dismounted helped Pythia into the saddle.

Then she and the King were riding as swiftly as they could towards the City.

Just before they reached the Palace the King said:

"The joke is everyone will think we were just amusing ourselves. But I am sure the story of your behaving like a 'ministering angel' will reach the City before nightfall!"

"I hope not," Pythia replied, "or I may be called upon to deliver countless babies and will have no time for anything else!"

The way she spoke made it sound amusing, and once again the King was laughing.

As he had foretold, there were several Deputations waiting.

Fortunately, because the King was with her, Pythia found she needed to say very little.

She only shook hands, smiled, and tried to understand the very broken English of some of the Members of Parliament.

She thought it would be tactless and perhaps unkind for her to reveal that she was conversant with their own language.

They had obviously made a determined effort to speak hers.

She was nevertheless tired, and so was the King, when finally the last Deputation left the Palace.

They had all made speeches which repeated each other over and over again.

"What is happening now?" Pythia asked as they walked together from the Council Chamber.

"I hardly dare to tell you," the King said, "but we have a dinner-party to which I was obliged to ask the Prime Minister and the Members of the Cabinet, more of my relations, and your Ambassador and his wife."

There was a little pause before Pythia said:

"I wish I could have been alone with you. There are so many things I want to ask you."

"Tomorrow is our Wedding Day," the King said, "and after that, with any luck, we shall be left alone."

He was wondering as he spoke whether he should suggest that they might go somewhere on a honeymoon.

It was something that had never crossed his mind before she arrived.

He had decided that immediately after the wedding he would contrive to see as little as possible of his English wife.

As if Pythia felt she was somehow pushing herself upon him, she said quickly:

"Of course, there is the wedding to get through first. And as I also have to be crowned, I only hope I do not do anything wrong."

"I am sure you will do everything right," the King said, "even if it is a little unexpected, like delivering a baby in the middle of the Cathedral!"

"Now you are being unkind," Pythia protested, "and you have to admit that at least, I have added to the population."

The King laughed as she ran up the stairs towards her bedroom.

*   *   *

After innumerable and endless speeches, the evening ended.

Pythia was not the only person who was tired, for so was the King.

He went to his own room.

Without even thinking of Natasha, he fell asleep as soon as his head touched the pillow.

*　　*　　*

When Pythia awoke the following morning she found it difficult to realise that this was her Wedding Day.

She thought that the King was very different from what she had expected.

She might have been shivering at being married to a man with whom she had nothing in common.

She was aware he rode superbly, and he had a sense of humour.

He was also, without doubt, the most handsome man she had ever seen.

'I am very fortunate, Papa,' she said in her head. 'I do not love him as Mama loved you, and I know he does not love me, but perhaps we have at least a small foundation on which to build a happy marriage.'

The more she saw of the Palace, the more she felt convinced it had been built for love.

It was so beautiful.

Flowers came in from the gardens every day and scented the air.

The sunshine coming through the windows dazzled her eyes.

She guessed that by now Princess Erina and Marcos's honeymoon would be coming to an end.

They would be thinking of going to Peru.

Then her aunt would be on her way there.

Pythia wondered if any of them would give even a thought as to how she was faring in a strange country with a husband who was wildly infatuated with a Russian Countess.

Although she knew it was indiscreet, she said to Aphaia:

"I understand there is a Russian lady staying in the Guest-House. Have you seen her?"

The maid gave her a quick perceptive glance before she replied:

"Yes, Your Highness."

"Is she beautiful?"

"Very beautiful," the maid replied, "but it is a beauty which comes from Satan, and not from God!"

Pythia did not ask any more. She understood.

Every nerve in her body was telling that she must save the King from something that was intrinsically wicked.

"How shall I do that, Papa?" she asked.

She could not have travelled as much as she had without learning there were women who enticed men away from their wives and families.

They were steeped in sin and often branded as Witches.

Because the Countess was Russian, she was sure that in some way she was dangerous, not only because she had seduced the King as a man but also because he was a King.

As always when she was deeply troubled, her thoughts went to Delphi.

She was ten years old when her father had taken her there.

He had shown her where she had been born in a little hut which now was only a ruin.

He had directed her eyes to the "Shining Cliffs."

He had told her why he had named her "Pythia" after the Priestess who spoke the words of the god.

"I am sure," Patrick O'Connor said, "that the Pythia who was the Priestess here will always guide and protect you, and if you call upon Apollo when you are in danger, he will come to you."

When Pythia was being dressed for her wedding, her thoughts kept returning to the Shining Cliffs.

She felt in a way she could not understand that the Light of Apollo was shining into her heart.

She wondered if the King had spent the night before with the beautiful Countess, and whether he was wishing he could marry her instead.

Pythia was praying, as the maids placed her veil on her head, that one day he would care for her not just a little, but with his whole heart.

Her wedding-gown was exquisitely lovely.

On her mother's instructions, it was simple compared to the very elaborately embroidered train which followed it.

This was to be carried by two young page-boys who were the sons of one of the King's cousins.

There were to be no adult bridesmaids.

Instead, behind the pages came six little girls all

dressed in pink, again relatives of the King.

When Pythia saw them she thought they looked like a bunch of roses.

She was very grateful to the Ambassadress.

It was the Ambassadress who had said that a large number of older girls would detract attention from the Bride.

They would also obstruct the view the congregation would otherwise have of the actual ceremony.

She had not at first realised how small and, in a way, fragile Pythia looked.

When she came to see her before she left for the Church, she exclaimed:

"You look beautiful, Your Highness! So young and innocent that you might be an angel instead of a Bride!"

"I would like to be both," Pythia said, "and thank you for your kindness, Your Excellency, in arranging everything so splendidly!"

"I only hope the children behave well," the Ambassadress said in a worried tone. "But they look so pretty that I am sure whatever they do will be forgiven."

"Of course it will," Pythia agreed.

The Ambassadress hesitated.

"Is it really true, my dear, as I have just heard, that you delivered a baby when you were out riding with His Majesty yesterday?"

"The woman had a fall and went into labour sooner than expected," Pythia explained. "There was nobody with her except her son of only six, and if I had not been there, the baby would have died."

"I can hardly believe it is true!" the Ambassadress said. "My maid tells me that everybody in the City is talking about what you did. I am sure it must be the first time a Queen has ever delivered a child!"

"We shall have to read the History Books to find out," Pythia said as she smiled. "I am only thankful that I knew what to do."

"I find it extraordinary that you did!" the Ambassadress replied.

Pythia thought that the less said about that, the better.

It was therefore a relief when a few moments later Major Danilo came to the door.

He told her that His Majesty had left for the Cathedral and the Ambassador was waiting downstairs to escort her there.

The Ambassadress hurried away to go ahead.

Having thanked the maids, Pythia walked beside Major Danilo towards the stairs.

"I suppose you realise," he said, "that you have already captured the hearts and the imaginations of all the women in the City by what you did yesterday?"

"It was certainly a surprise," Pythia replied. "I only hope there are no more today!"

"You know I am here if you need me," Major Danilo said in a low voice.

She wondered why he was speaking like that, but there was no time to ask questions.

As she came down the stairs the Ambassador was waiting for her.

The footmen in the hall gazed at her as if she were a being from another Planet.

The pages and bridesmaids had gone ahead in one of the State Carriages to await her arrival at the Cathedral door.

The open carriage in which Pythia and the Ambassador were to travel was drawn by two white horses decorated with garlands of flowers.

There were also a few flowers on the open hood.

They drove down the long road which led from the Palace to the Cathedral.

As they did so, children crept between the soldiers who were lining the route.

They ran up to the carriage to throw flowers into it.

They were the wild flowers over which Pythia had ridden the day before.

She smiled at the children and waved at the crowds.

They had gathered on either side of the road to see her pass.

As she did so, she felt everything happening was an omen for happiness.

She need no longer fear for the future.

There were cheers when she arrived at the Cathedral.

As she walked up the steps the women shouted:

"Good luck! God bless you!"

Inside the West Door the pages were waiting to take up her train.

The bridesmaids in their pink dresses were grouped behind them.

They were so excited at being part of such an important occasion that they forgot to walk in pairs.

They huddled together like a posy of flowers as Pythia moved up the aisle.

The Cathedral was packed with the King's relatives, rich landowners, the Dignitaries of the City, down to the peasants.

Many of them were poorly dressed and had travelled miles to squeeze in at the back.

The King in full regalia looked magnificent.

Pythia peeped at him through her veil.

She saw that he was not looking bored, as she had feared, nor was he frowning.

The Marriage Service was a long and impressive one.

Finally after they were married Pythia knelt before the King.

He placed the Queen's crown on her head.

As he did so, she prayed that she might do everything that was right for Vultarnia, that with the King's help she would make it much more prosperous than it was at the moment.

It was a very poignant prayer. In her heart she said:

"Please, God, help me . . . please!"

Then for a moment she felt the Light of Apollo blinding her eyes and she could see nothing else.

The crown was on her head and she was Queen of Vultarnia.

* * *

As they drove back to the Palace in the State Coach drawn by six white horses, the cheers of the crowds were deafening.

Once again the children could not be stopped from running beside them.

It seemed as if the flowers had multiplied while they were being married.

Now they almost covered them.

It was impossible to speak above the cheers.

But because she was so moved by such an enthusiastic reception, she slipped her free hand into the King's.

She continued to wave with the other.

As his fingers closed over hers, she felt that he protected her, although from whom or what she was not sure.

They walked up the steps to the Palace.

Pythia's train spread out behind her, but the crowds could not follow them.

Soldiers barred their way.

When the King and Pythia made it to the top, they turned back to wave.

They stood there for some little time before they entered the Palace, only to be called back while the Reception was taking place.

"I have never known your people to be so enthusiastic!" one of the King's relatives observed.

"They are cheering their new Queen—not me!" the King replied.

Pythia hoped this was not true, but she had the uncomfortable feeling that it was.

'I have to help him,' she thought.

Once again it was difficult to know how to do so.

They did not sit down to the Banquet until nearly four o'clock.

There was a great deal to eat and drink and a

great number of speeches to listen to.

Before that the King and his Queen had received their guests.

They filed past one by one, including a number of Ambassadors from other countries of the Balkans.

To the King's astonishment he heard Pythia speaking to each one in their own language.

At first he thought he must be mistaken.

Then he heard her asking a Romanian about horses in his country, and speaking in Serbian to the Ambassador of that country.

He thought it extraordinary.

He had, because of her father, expected her to be at ease with their guests who came from Greece.

But he had never imagined she would know any other Balkan languages.

Admittedly she might have come in contact with quite a number of people when Prince Lucian was in Seriphos.

He reasoned, however, that she had not been very old at the time.

From what he had learnt, Princess Aileen, after she was widowed, had been very poor.

She had also been of no particular importance in England.

How had the Queen learnt so much?

"She is certainly most unusual," he mused, "and not in the least what I had expected."

She turned her head for a moment to smile at him.

He thought it was impossible for anyone to be more lovely.

At the same time, she had an unmistakable aura of purity about her.

It was something he had never encountered before in any woman.

But that was hardly surprising considering the type of women with whom he had spent his time when he wandered around the world.

Everything about this girl seemed like magic.

He was vividly conscious of her in a very different way from how he had been conscious of women in the past.

Then there had been a fiery rapport which had drawn them physically together.

He had, however, always known it was a feeling that would not last.

Usually, after a very short time, he was, in his own words, "off to pastures new."

Now he was acutely aware of his Bride standing beside him.

He thought she was somehow like the butterflies that had fluttered before them when they had galloped yesterday morning.

She was just as fragile, just as beautiful, and, at the same time, difficult to capture and hold.

He could not understand why such thoughts should come to him.

Yet they were there all the time he was receiving one guest after another.

He was thanking them for their congratulations, which he knew were completely sincere.

Only when the last speech had been made and the last toast drunk did the King say quietly to Pythia:

"Only a little while longer, then we can relax!"

"I shall be glad to take off my tiara," she replied. "It is very heavy!"

She had taken off her crown and her train after the reception.

But the tiara she had put on instead was brilliant with large diamonds and was quite a weight.

"I remember my mother always said the same thing," the King was saying, "and I think what we will do is go upstairs to your *Boudoir* and put up our feet."

"That sounds delightful!" Pythia exclaimed.

As she spoke, Major Danilo came to the King's side to say in a low voice:

"I am afraid, Your Majesty, there is trouble outside!"

chapter six

"TROUBLE?" the King exclaimed.

"Yes, Your Majesty, and I think it would be wise if you came outside."

The King rose to his feet and Pythia did the same.

He did not say anything, and the guests at the table watched him go, wondering if they should follow.

However, Major Danilo made a gesture to them not to move and they obeyed him.

When the King left the Dining-Room he walked quickly towards the front Hall.

Now Pythia could hear shouts and yells coming from outside the Palace.

There were a number of people in the Hall, including the Servants at the door.

As it was made mostly of glass, those in the Hall could see through it.

There were also large windows on either side.

"What has happened?" the King asked Major Danilo.

"The young element in the City, who have been causing trouble for some time," Major Danilo replied, "have come here to protest against the money spent on the wedding when they are out of work and have to go without food."

The King frowned.

Pythia, walking towards the door, could see that in front of the Palace and even standing on the steps there was a huge crowd.

There were gesticulating and shouting and were held back from proceeding any further only by a line of soldiers.

She looked at them for the best part of a minute and the King did the same without speaking.

Then an *Aide-de-Camp* behind him said:

"The General has just arrived, Your Majesty."

The King turned away to speak to the General.

At that moment, almost as if a voice were telling her what to do, Pythia knew this was her opportunity.

She said to Major Danilo in a low voice:

"I am going out to speak to them. Do not let anyone follow me."

He stared at her in consternation, and she said:

"I know it is right. Open the door!"

For a moment her eyes met his.

As if he realised that she was being moved by a greater force than her own, he acquiesced.

He opened the door just enough for her to move through it, then shut it again.

She walked to the top of the steps.

When she reached the soldiers she gave an order:

"Move to one side!"

They turned to look at her in astonishment, but slowly did as she wanted.

Now the crowd could see her.

Because she was higher than they were, the people who were massed on the steps and below them on the road could see that she stood alone.

Her tiara was glittering on her head and her bridal gown made her look very ethereal and at the same time very lovely.

As the last soldier made way for her, there was complete silence.

It was then that Pythia lifted her voice, and she felt as if she were being told exactly what to say.

"People of Vultarnia," she began. "I am now your Queen. I want to bring to your beautiful country many things, and above all what you are asking for—changes!"

There was a gasp from the crowd. Then a man shouted:

"That's what we want—changes—and for the better!"

"And you are quite right to want them," Pythia said. "Yesterday, as some of you may have heard, I delivered a baby boy, and as I did so I thought that we must make this City and the country as a whole a better place for him to grow up in."

"How can we do that with no work?" a man half-way down the steps demanded.

"That is what I am going to tell you," Pythia

replied. "But I am going to speak first to the women of Vultarnia, because I know they will understand what I am about to say."

Pythia could see a number of women in the crowd, most of them at the bottom of the steps or in the road.

Raising her voice so that they could hear her, she said:

"I want the women of the City to help me, first to build a Hospital, then good Schools for our children. We have to make every child in this country clever enough to compete with our neighbours, and even the countries farther afield in the Mediterranean."

She smiled at them before she continued:

"We women know also that we should have for our children more and better food than is available at the moment in Vultarnia."

She paused for a moment.

Then the man who she thought must be the leader of the demonstration and was standing on the step below her asked:

"And what do we use for money?"

It was then Pythia was aware that the King was beside her.

He had followed her out almost as soon as she began to speak.

He had stood just behind her until now he came to her side.

"My wife is right," he said in a voice that all those listening could hear, "and I can only apologise to you all that I did not realise before how much there is to be done in our country. But it is not too late."

He paused a moment and then went on:

"I intend to have a strong Army, and I hope many of you younger men who have no families or responsibilities of that sort will join in helping me to raise more troops and have better guns and better equipment with which to fight for our freedom should the necessity arise."

There was a little murmur as if most of those listening knew to what he was referring.

"You have already heard the Queen say that you must have better food," the King went on. "Now, all of you are aware that Vultarnia has much excellent land which lies uncultivated. I intend to give every married man in the City two acres of land so that he can cultivate it and sell any crops in excess of what he requires for his own family."

There was now a loud murmur of excitement from the crowd as the King continued:

"There are many among you who are interested in caring for animals. Very well—any man who applies to me will receive a number of goats, sheep, or cows with which to start his own flock or herd."

The people began to cheer at this, but the King held up his hand for silence as he went on:

"The question was asked of the Queen—how are we to pay for the Hospital, the Schools, and all the other things that need doing. I will tell you. I intend to send to Greece, Italy, and France for experts who will find out if there are any minerals to be found in our mountains which will create for us the financial base we need."

He smiled before he said:

"When I was a boy I thought they were full of gold, but I think there may be other minerals which are just as valuable and just as necessary not only to us, but to all the Balkan countries and many other countries in the world."

His voice rose a little as he finished:

"While these investigations are taking place, which will, of course, take time, I will pay every unemployed man in Vultarnia who can work as a carpenter, a painter, or, if he is experienced enough, as a builder."

He paused before he went on:

"I want our Capital City to be worthy of its beautiful Queen."

As he finished speaking he took Pythia's hand and raised it to his lips.

It was then the cheers rang out.

The loudest of them all coming, Pythia noticed, from the man nearest to her whom she was certain had started the demonstration.

It was then her fingers tightened on the King's, and she drew him forward.

He realised what she intended.

They walked down the steps, shaking hands with the rioters, who were too astonished to say anything.

They could only stand and stare at them.

When they reached the bottom of the steps, the women clustered round Pythia.

They talked excitedly about the baby she had

delivered the previous day and how the mother could hardly believe it had happened.

"You will have to help me," Pythia said to them. "I know you will help me to build a really fine Hospital."

"It's be a gift from Heaven," one woman answered. "There be only three Doctors in Vultarnia, and they goes only to them as can pay."

"Then I will arrange for Doctors to be always on duty at certain hours," Pythia said, "and everyone who goes to them will be treated free of charge."

As she spoke, one woman burst into tears.

Going down on her knees, she kissed the hem of Pythia's gown.

"You're an angel sent by God to help us!" she sobbed.

Pythia must have shaken hands with hundreds of people before the King said to those crowded round them:

"You will understand that the Queen is tired. It has been a long day, but a very happy one. God bless you all!"

He turned with Pythia as he spoke, and they walked up the steps, the crowds cheering wildly behind them.

When they reached the top they found standing outside the front-door the Prime Minister and a number of other guests from the Banquet.

They had been watching what was happening in sheer astonishment.

As the King and Pythia joined them, the Prime Minister said:

"I can never remember, Your Majesty, anything

like this ever happening before!"

"I have the feeling, Prime Minister," the King replied, "that you will have a similar experience many times in the future."

He paused and smiled before he continued:

"Now we have to put our heads together and borrow enough money to pay for everything that has been suggested until this country is utilising all its underdeveloped assets, as it should have done a long time ago."

Pythia thought the Members of the Cabinet looked somewhat guilty.

The King took her into the Palace, where his relatives were waiting to congratulate them.

Then at last everybody left and finally Pythia and the King could go upstairs.

They went, as he had suggested, to her *Boudoir*.

It was a very attractive room opening out of her bedroom.

She had hardly had time to look at it because there had been so much to do.

She had seemed to be in a constant hurry ever since she had arrived.

She sank down on the sofa.

The King walked to a table on which there was a bottle of champagne in a gold ice-cooler.

"I think we have earned a drink," he said, "and if your throat is not dry, mine is!"

Pythia was busy taking off her tiara which she then put down on a side-table.

She patted her hair into place.

The King put a glass of champagne into her

hand before he sat down in a chair beside her sofa and said:

"Now tell me how it is you can speak my language perfectly, and why you did not tell me you could do so."

"Major Danilo has been an excellent teacher," Pythia replied, "and it is also very like the languages of the other Balkan countries and specially of Greece."

She knew that was a reasonable explanation, and the King said:

"I am completely astonished by what you did just now. I can only say that if you do many more such unexpected things, I shall have a heart attack!"

She laughed.

"That is unlikely, and I think your ideas are splendid and exactly what is wanted."

"It was you who made me realise that what is wrong can be put right," the King replied. "I am painfully aware that I have been very remiss in not knowing this before."

"Do not let us waste our time in looking back," Pythia pleaded. "That was yesterday, and we have a Herculean task waiting for us tomorrow."

The King laughed.

"That is the right word, but I am quite certain you will achieve all you have set out to do."

"Not without you," Pythia said quietly. "This is your country."

Their eyes met, and somehow it was difficult to look away.

Then the King said:

"Before we step into tomorrow, you will not have forgotten that tonight is our wedding-night?"

Pythia's eye-lashes flickered, and she could not look at him as she said in a low voice:

"I . . . I had not . . . forgotten."

He did not speak, and after a moment she said:

"There is . . . something I would like to . . . say to you."

There was a little pause before the King answered:

"I am listening."

"I . . . I know that our . . . marriage was one of . . . convenience," Pythia began in a very small voice, "and because you . . . applied to Queen Victoria for . . . help in . . . providing Vultarnia with an English . . . Queen . . . there was no question of the person . . . chosen for the position . . . being able . . . to refuse."

"It was something my Cabinet forced me to do," the King said, "and I will be frank with you and tell you that I had no wish to marry, and if I did, I would have preferred to choose my own bride."

"Of course," Pythia agreed. "I entirely . . . understand your feelings. And I, for my part, wanted to . . . marry a man . . . I loved."

"You were not attracted by the idea of wearing a crown?" the King asked.

Pythia shook her head.

"All I wanted was . . . love . . . the real love that my . . . father and mother had for each other."

"But now we are married," the King pointed out, "and there is nothing either of us can do about the situation, although it is a very different one from what I expected."

He put down his glass of champagne, and sitting forward, said in a very deep voice:

"You are very beautiful, Erina. In fact, so beautiful that it would be impossible for any man not to want to possess you and make you his!"

He saw the colour flood into Pythia's cheeks.

He thought it made her even more enchanting.

"What I am trying to say," the King went on, "is that I want you as a woman. I think when we get to know each other better we shall be very happy."

Now there was undoubtedly an expression in his eyes that had not been there before.

It made Pythia feel very shy.

With an effort she said:

"I have . . . thought about this . . . and there is . . . something more I . . . have to . . . say to . . . you."

"Then you must know it is something I want to hear," the King said.

"I . . . I have already . . . told you," Pythia said a little hesitatingly, "that . . . I want . . . love . . . and I think it . . . would be very . . . easy . . . if you want it . . . for me to . . . love you."

She drew in her breath before she continued in a voice he could hardly hear:

"But . . . I know you are . . . in love with . . . somebody else . . . and I can only . . . hope that . . . perhaps one day . . . if we wait . . . you will begin to . . . love me."

They were brave words which Pythia found it difficult to say.

As she finished speaking the King rose to his feet. He walked across to the window as if he wanted to breathe in the fresh air.

There was silence until he asked without turning round:

"I suppose you have been told about the Russian Countess who is my guest!"

"I . . . overheard a . . . conversation when I was . . . aboard the ship . . . carrying me here," Pythia said, "and . . . I understand . . . of course I understand . . . that as she is very beautiful . . . and you were . . . alone . . . she was what you . . . wanted."

The King still did not turn round.

He was thinking, and it was, in fact, a strange thing for him to think, that he hoped his wife, with her purity and innocence, would never come in contact with Natasha.

He felt he could not bear her to know how wild and exotic their love-making was.

Above all things, he did not want her to be shocked.

Then a voice behind him said:

"Please . . . do not be angry . . . or think it presumptuous of me to . . . speak to you of this . . . but everything in your country is . . . so beautiful that I could not . . . bear to spoil it."

The King knew exactly what she was trying to say.

It would spoil it for her if she thought that having given his heart to another woman he should make love to her simply because it was his duty, and she was his legal wife.

He felt he could read her thoughts.

He knew they were as spiritual and ethereal as she was herself.

A hasty word, a hasty gesture, might frighten and perhaps appal her.

Like her, he had no wish to spoil anything so perfect.

He turned round.

"I am not in the least angry," he said. "In fact, I think, Erina, that you are a very remarkable and very wonderful young woman."

He paused a moment before continuing:

"When you went out alone to face that shouting crowd I was terrified lest anything should happen to you. I had the greatest difficulty in making Major Danilo let me out to stand beside you."

"I . . . I told him not to . . . let anybody . . . through," Pythia explained.

"And of course he obeyed you rather than his Monarch to whom he has sworn allegiance!"

"You are . . . not annoyed . . . with him?" Pythia asked quickly.

The King shook his head.

"He knew better than I did that you were doing the right thing. But then, of course, he has known you longer."

"I believe what you said will make the whole City happy," Pythia remarked.

"What *you* said," the King corrected her, "and I can only thank you again for showing me the right way to rule over my people, which is something I should have known for myself this past year."

Pythia held up her hands.

"Now you are looking back again," she said, "but I am thinking of tomorrow. I know there will be a lot of exciting things to do, if only it is watching the first coat of paint being applied to one of the houses."

She smiled at him as she went on:

"And I hope somebody will put the glass back in the windows of the Cathedral!"

The King laughed again.

"How can you be so fantastic?" he asked. "You have just quelled a revolution single-handed, and now you are worrying about the glass in the Cathedral windows!"

He laughed again and Pythia laughed too.

"It does sound absurd when you put it like that, but it is the little things in life that matter. Who would have imagined when we rode before breakfast that I would have to deliver a baby, which ensured that all the women in the City are on my side?"

"I too am on your side," the King said, "if you will allow me to be."

Once again their eyes met. Pythia had the strange feeling that if she made the slightest movement, he would take her in his arms.

But a voice within her seemed to be telling her that it was too soon.

They must both wait.

She was sure she would know the right moment when it came, or Apollo would show her the way.

The King stood looking down at her. Then he said:

"I want you now to go to bed. You are tired,

and, as you say, tomorrow will be an exciting day when we shall have a lot to do together."

"I will do as you say," Pythia said. "The Banquet went on for so long and so much has happened after it that it is actually already bedtime."

"Then all I can ask," the King said, "is that you dream of me, and I am quite certain I shall be dreaming of you."

Pythia held out both hands and he drew her to her feet.

Just for a moment they stood looking at each other.

Then he kissed first one hand, then the other, his lips lingering on the softness of her skin.

She felt something like a little shaft of lightning streak through her breast.

Because it made her shy, she turned towards the communicating door which was in one corner of the room.

The King opened it for her.

As he did so she said softly:

"Thank you, and I know that God has blessed us both and we are very, very lucky."

She was thinking of the demonstration, but the King was looking at her as he said:

"Very lucky indeed, and I am more grateful than I can ever say."

She smiled at him and he shut the door.

He did not go at once to his own bedroom. He helped himself to another glass of champagne and sat down in the chair he had occupied before.

He was making a decision, and it was, in fact, not a very difficult one.

It was that he must tell Natasha to leave the Palace.

He knew now it was something he should most certainly have done before his marriage took place.

In fact, he should have done it as soon as he learnt that Queen Victoria had acceded to his request and a Princess was leaving almost immediately in a Battle ship.

He thought that any other woman except his wife would have considered it a gross insult that she should be brought to the Palace when his mistress was still staying there.

"I must have been mad," the King chided himself, "to have behaved in such an outrageous manner!"

Once again he was thinking that this lovely, unspoilt child must never know the way he had behaved with Natasha and a great many other women in his life.

For her, love was something Divine which came from God. She had no idea of the perversions and vices which were practised in the name of Love, but were in fact nothing but lust.

He had often told himself that love was only a dream expressed by Poets and Musicians.

There would always be men like himself who must be content with passion. It was very satisfying for the moment, even if it did not last.

Now he was aware, as he had never been before, that the love which this young girl envisaged so clearly was as spiritual and beautiful as her soul.

It was as pure and unspoilt as her body.

"I want her as a woman," he told himself, "and

God knows, I would be inhuman if she did not attract me."

At the same time, he understood exactly what she wanted from him.

It was his heart and his soul, although he was not quite certain if he possessed one.

It was something he had never given to any woman. Yet he knew that his wife would be content with nothing less.

It was a long time later when the King walked from the *Boudoir* into his own room, which was on the other side of it.

His Valet was waiting for him, but when he was about to take off his decorations, the man said:

"There's a note just come for Your Majesty, which I was told was very urgent, and must be attended to immediately."

He handed it to the King on a gold salver, and one glance told him whom it was from.

Quite suddenly he had no desire to open it.

He did not want at this particular moment to have Natasha intruding upon him in any way.

As he picked up the note from the salver he had an impulse to tear it into pieces and throw it into the waste-paper basket.

His Valet knew he was hesitating, and almost as if he could read his master's thoughts, he said:

"I was told it was urgent, Your Majesty, but I didn't like to disturb you when you were with the Queen."

Impatiently the King opened the note.

To his surprise it consisted of only a few lines, and he read:

*Come to me quickly, I am desperate! I must
speak to you.*

Natasha.

He read it over twice and thought that something unforeseen must have occurred.

He could not believe she would disturb him
on his wedding-night if she was not, as she had
described it, desperate.

He could not imagine what it could be. But he
told himself he owed it to her at least to listen to
what she had to say.

At the same time, he would tell her that she had
to leave the Palace and that he could not see her
again.

He supposed she would make a fuss. There
would be the usual tears and recriminations he
had experienced before with quite a number of
other women.

Putting the note in his pocket, he walked down
the corridor. He was thinking as he went that it
was really reprehensible of Natasha to contact him
tonight, of all nights.

*   *   *

Pythia found Aphaia waiting for her in her bedroom. As the maid took off her gown and she put
on a nightgown, she realised she was, in fact,
physically exhausted.

But she admitted too that she was excited by all
that had taken place.

When Aphaia had gone and she was alone,

Pythia whispered to her father:

"I *have* helped Vultarnia, Papa. Now the King will be interested in ruling over his people, and we will make this the happiest Kingdom in the whole of the Balkans!"

She felt she could see her father smiling at her and hear his laughter as if he was delighted at what she had done.

Then she fell asleep.

*   *   *

Pythia was dreaming of the King when she was aware that somebody had knocked on her door.

As she stirred and wondered what it could be, the door opened. Somebody carrying a candle came into the room.

She thought for a moment it must be the King.

Then she was aware that whoever had entered had done so by way of the door leading from the corridor.

"W-what is it?" she asked.

"Forgive me for waking you, Your Majesty," Major Danilo said, "but there is a monk here from the Monastery who says he must see you urgently. He has been sent by the Abbot, and he says it is a matter of life and death!"

Pythia remembered how the Abbot had said he would help her, should the occasion arise.

"I will come at once!" she said.

Major Danilo did not say any more.

He merely put down the candle he was carrying in his hand onto the bedside table, and went out into the corridor, leaving the door ajar.

Pythia got out of bed and picked up her negligée which Aphaia had left lying over a chair.

It was a very beautiful garment which had come from Bond Street.

Made of satin and lace, it had been, like the rest of her trousseau, very expensive.

She put it on, and slid her feet into her soft, heelless velvet slippers. She went to the door without stopping to look in the mirror.

She knew that if the Abbot had sent a monk with a message that meant "life or death," that was exactly what it was.

Major Danilo was waiting outside, and now he had another candle in his hand.

She realised he had taken it from one of the sconces on the walls.

"Where is the monk?" she asked in a whisper.

"He is in the small Waiting-Room downstairs," he replied. "If we go down a secondary staircase, nobody will see you."

He set off at a pace which meant that Pythia was almost running beside him.

She knew that he was definitely worried and agitated about what the monk had to impart.

They went down the staircase, and only as they moved down the main corridor did Major Danilo say:

"The man is exhausted, but he will speak to no-one but you."

He opened the door as he spoke. Pythia went into a small Waiting-Room, where seated in a chair was a monk who she thought was having difficulty in breathing.

As she reached his side and he would have risen, she put a hand on his shoulder and said:

"No, do not move. Just give me the message you have come to deliver."

She saw as she spoke that he was far from being a young man.

She guessed that the monk was Vultarnian. The Abbot had sent him because he would know the way.

"They are—just behind me!" the monk began with an effort. "I managed to—pass them and—get here first. There is—little time in which to—save His Majesty!"

"Who are they, and what are they planning?" Pythia asked.

"They are Russians who arrived late last night after their ship had had difficulty entering the Port. One of our monks who speaks Russian heard them say that they intended to—kidnap the King and—take him to Russia!"

Pythia gave a stifled exclamation of horror, and the monk went on:

"They will seize him and take him from the Palace tonight, and no one will know where they have gone except for the Countess Zarlinski, who will go with him."

Pythia drew in her breath.

Then she looked at Major Danilo standing beside her.

"Where is His Majesty?" she asked.

"I saw him as I was on my way to you," Major Danilo replied. "He was going towards the Guest-House."

"Then we must go there," Pythia said.

She turned to the monk.

"How many Russians are there?" she enquired.

"Four," the monk answered, "and they are dangerous—Your Highness—very dangerous!"

His voice died away, and he shut his eyes as if it had all been too much for him.

Pythia ran across the room to the door, and Major Danilo followed her.

As he went outside he saw one of the senior Servants looking at Pythia in surprise.

"There is a monk in the Waiting-Room," Major Danilo told the man. "He is exhausted after a difficult journey. Look after him until I return, and see that he is given food and wine."

He spoke sharply and did not wait for the Servant to reply.

Pythia was already half-way down the corridor, and he ran after her.

She knew where the Guest-House was, but had not been anywhere near it.

As Major Danilo joined her, they hurried down passage after passage.

Pythia was almost breathless as she reached it, but she realised with relief that everything was very quiet.

Some of the candles in the sconces had been extinguished.

There were three, however, in a sconce opposite

a door half-way down the passage.

It was towards that door that Major Danilo now hurried.

She wondered what they would do if it was locked.

To her relief, however, she saw him take a master key from his pocket, but there was no need for it.

When he turned the handle the door opened.

He stood aside to let Pythia enter, and she found herself in a luxuriously furnished Sitting-Room.

With a constriction of her heart she realised the King was not there.

Then she heard his voice from the next room.

As the door of it was open, she had a quick glimpse of a large canopied bed before she saw him.

He was fully dressed and standing talking, she thought, somewhat aggressively.

Stretched out on a divan was the most beautiful woman Pythia had ever seen.

Her long, dark hair flowed over her shoulders, and she was wearing only a diaphanous, transparent nightgown.

It was the same colour as the emeralds round her throat.

They were speaking in French and did not realise Pythia was standing in the doorway.

She took two hesitant steps forward before the King exclaimed:

"Erina! What are you doing here?"

For a moment Pythia did not know what to reply.

Then, as if once again she was being prompted, the words came to her lips.

"Something . . . terrible has happened!" she said. "A man has brought you a very . . . important . . . message, but he is . . . dying and unless you . . . hurry he will be . . . dead before you can . . . hear what he has . . . to say!"

The King stared at her and the Countess asked petulantly:

"What is all this? Why has the Queen come to my apartment?"

Pythia realised that because she and the King had spoken to each other in English, the Countess had not understood.

"I will come at once," the King said.

"Thank you . . . but please . . . please hurry," Pythia begged. "He will not tell . . . anyone but . . . you!"

She moved towards the door and the King followed her.

The Countess sprang to her feet.

"This is ridiculous!" she exclaimed. "You cannot leave me, Alexius! I want you! I need you badly!"

"That is untrue," the King replied, "but I will come back later and tell you what *I* have to say."

He accentuated the pronoun.

By now Pythia had reached the outer door.

The Countess clutched hold of the King's arm.

"Stay with me, Alexius! I have to see you!"

The King shook himself free.

"Behave yourself!" he commanded.

"You will return?"

"If it is possible."

He went through the outer door and shut it behind him.

Pythia was out in the corridor, but there was no sign of Major Danilo.

She turned to look in the opposite direction to that from which they had come.

She could make out his figure standing in the shadows where he must have dimmed the lights.

He made a gesture with his hand.

She understood he was telling her that the Russians were approaching.

She therefore hurried the King to the other end of the corridor towards the stairs.

When she reached it she stopped.

"Wait one moment," she said in a whisper.

As she spoke she blew out the candles which had illuminated that part of the passage so that they were now in darkness.

As she looked back she saw a movement where Major Danilo had been.

She caught hold of the King and drew him out of sight.

At the same time, he could see, as she could, a man who was now making his way down the corridor.

He was going towards the door of the room they had just left.

He was walking on tip-toe, his back bent, as if he wished to conceal himself.

He was followed by another man, then two more.

The King understood that he must remain silent.

He moved only a little in the darkness so that he could see more clearly.

Now he was peeking back into the corridor, as Pythia was.

It was obvious to her that the four newcomers were Russians.

They stood for a moment outside the door.

Then three of the men drew long-bladed knives, which gleamed in the candlelight, from their waists.

The fourth man carried a rope under his arm.

The first Russian knocked softly on the door, and instantly it was opened.

For a moment the King stiffened.

He thought that Natasha was in danger and he must save her.

In the candlelight they could see her quite clearly, and now it was obvious that she was not afraid.

She was, in fact, beckoning to the men to enter her room, gesticulating with her hands as she did so.

Pythia did not understand Russian.

She was, however, quite certain the Countess was telling them that the King had gone but would come back.

The Russians followed her into the room and the door was shut behind them.

It was then that Pythia felt she had been holding her breath.

She was sure the King had been doing the same.

Major Danilo came hurrying towards them.

He did not speak, but motioned to the King to go down the stairs.

He did so, Pythia following, until when they reached the lighted corridor below, Major Danilo said:

"Her Majesty has saved you, Sire, by two minutes! I was desperately afraid they would see you leaving the apartment!"

Pythia looked up at the King.

She saw that his chin was squared and his lips were closed in a hard line.

"How did those men get into the Palace?" he demanded.

"I am afraid they have killed the sentry, Your Majesty, who was on duty at the side door."

"Take soldiers and arrest them immediately!" the King said. "And charge them with murder and attempted burglary!"

"Yes, Your Majesty!"

"Also have the Countess escorted under armed guard to the border. Tell the Officer in Charge to make it quite clear to her that if she ever enters Vultarnia again, she will be arrested and imprisoned."

Major Danilo saluted.

Pythia saw the glint in his eyes that told her how delighted he was at the order.

They walked on and the King said:

"Is there really somebody to see me?"

"There is indeed," Pythia replied. "One of the monks was sent by the Abbot from the Monastery to warn you that the Russians had arrived there from the Port where a Russian ship is waiting to take you away to Russia."

She saw the anger in the King's face and added in a voice he could hardly hear:

"The . . . Countess was to have . . . gone with you."

As she spoke they reached the room where the monk was waiting.

As the King opened the door she could see he was sitting at a table.

He was obviously enjoying the food that had been set in front of him.

There was also a bottle of wine.

When he saw the King, the monk rose a little unsteadily to his feet.

"Your Majesty is safe!" he exclaimed.

"Safe, thanks to you," the King answered, "and I am very grateful to you, and also to your Abbot."

Pythia felt sure that the King would send the Monastery a generous donation.

She thought she was no longer needed.

For the first time she felt a little embarrassed by the scanty way she was dressed.

She therefore went from the Waiting-Room.

She hurried back alone up the staircase down which the Major had brought her.

She reached her own room without being seen.

Only then did she realise that if she had not been informed, the King would by now have been carried away as a prisoner of the four Russians.

Because she was so grateful, she went down on her knees.

Kneeling by the bed, she said a prayer of gratitude to God, to her father, and to Apollo.

She felt they had all been instrumental in saving the King's life.

"Thank you . . . thank you . . ." she said over and over again.

The words seemed to tumble from her lips.

She knew then that she loved the King.

chapter seven

THE King listened attentively to everything the Monk told him.

He knew better than Pythia what would have happened if he had been kidnapped from the Palace.

He would have been taken to the ship that was waiting in the harbour of Catarro.

Then, as far as Vultarnia was concerned, he would have disappeared for ever.

As Natasha was involved, he might be kept alive for a little while.

He would have been a close prisoner with no possibility of making any communication with the outside world.

After that he would be the victim of a convenient accident.

The whole operation had been carefully

planned so that it would take place before he could give his Bride a child.

This meant there would be no direct heir to the throne of Vultarnia.

Because of that, it would have been very easy for the country to be taken over.

There was no need to ask by whom.

It was all so clever that he found it hard to believe that only by a hair's breadth and Pythia's courage had he been able to escape.

He could imagine no other woman being brave enough to fetch him from his mistress's room just before the Russians arrived.

Anyone else would have been too shy to do so herself.

In which case precious moments would have been wasted while somebody else was sent to Natasha's apartment.

Then he would still have been there when the abductors arrived.

This all flashed through the King's mind while the monk was talking.

When the story was finished, the monk explained how difficult it had been to overtake the Russians.

Only by stumbling down the side of the mountains and running a head of them did he manage it.

"I can never thank you enough for your kindness and your courage in coming here," the King said. "I want you to spend a comfortable night here before you think of returning."

The Monk's face lit up at the idea of staying in

the Palace, and the King went on:

"As I am sure your feet are sore after what you have endured, I will send you tomorrow by carriage back to the Monastery, and you will carry back with you a gift for the Abbot of which I am sure he can make good use."

The Monk bowed almost to the ground as he murmured:

"God will reward Your Majesty."

"He has already done so," the King replied.

As he spoke, he realised that Pythia was no longer in the room as he had thought her to be.

He therefore left.

He found a senior Servant on duty outside.

He gave instructions that the Monk was to be given a comfortable bedroom in which to spend two or three nights.

"I wish to see him before he leaves," the King continued, "and he will travel in a carriage which will take him back to his Monastery."

The Servant bowed to show he understood the order.

The King then walked up the stairs.

As he did so, he realised it was very hot.

Impatiently he pulled off his white tunic and carried it over his arm.

He thought Pythia would be waiting for him in her *Boudoir*.

He felt sure she would want to discuss with him the drama in which they had both been involved.

He supposed she had gone away so quickly because she was embarrassed at the way she was dressed.

It struck him again that no-one else would have been so unselfconscious as to go to see the Monk straight from her bed.

Then she had gone to fetch him without being embarrassed because she was wearing her nightclothes.

As he walked along the corridor he knew he was eager to see her.

Yet, to his astonishment, when he opened the door of the *Boudoir* the room was in darkness.

The only light came from the communicating door which led to Pythia's room which was not completely closed.

The King threw his tunic down on a chair.

Then he manoeuvred his way through the darkness by the slit of light coming from the bedroom.

He pushed open the door.

Pythia was kneeling beside the bed in prayer.

The King stood still, looking at her and thinking that nothing could be more beautiful.

He could not remember when he had last seen a woman at prayer, except conventionally in Church.

Pythia had taken off her negligée.

She was wearing only the fine lace-trimmed nightgown that went beneath it.

The palms of her hands were pressed together.

As if she was speaking to God, her head was lifted up, although her eyes were closed.

The King did not move.

But as if Pythia were instinctively aware of him, she turned her head towards him.

Then, as if he had come in answer to her prayers,

she rose to her feet and ran across the room towards him.

As she reached him she said:

"You are safe . . . safe . . . and it was only by . . . two minutes that you were not . . . snatched . . . away by those . . . terrible men! I am so . . . grateful . . . so very . . . grateful to . . . God."

Her voice was almost incoherent.

The King saw there were tears in her eyes because of the intensity of her feelings.

"I also am very grateful to Him," he said in a deep voice, "and to you!"

"B-but . . . they may . . . try again!" she murmured.

"Would it matter to you if they did?" he asked.

"Of course . . . it would!" she replied. "But . . . God will protect you . . . He must . . . He must!"

Now there was a frantic note in her voice.

"I know He will do that," the King said.

As he spoke he put out his arms and pulled her against him.

For a moment she hardly realised what he was doing.

She only clung to him, then, lifting her face to his, she asked:

"What . . . can . . . we do? Have . . . you enough . . . soldiers?"

"I have you!" the King said, and his lips came down on hers.

He surprised her, but then he felt the quiver that went through her body and held her closer still.

Her lips were just as he expected them to be: soft, innocent, and untouched.

He was trying to be very gentle.

He knew that he had to protect her not only from anything that might hurt her, but also from himself.

It was then that Pythia felt a streak of lightning pass through her.

It was intense, and indescribable, yet almost as pain.

She had never dreamt that she would ever feel anything quite so perfect or so wonderful.

At the same time, there was a light that seemed to envelop both the King and herself.

She knew it was the Light of Apollo.

The King kissed her until slightly unsteadily he asked:

"How is it possible that I can feel like this?"

"I . . . I love you!"

There was a rapturous note in Pythia's voice that was like the song of the birds.

"And I love you!" the King said. "I know now that I loved you from the first moment I saw you, but I did not believe my own feelings."

"But you . . . do love . . . me?"

"I love and adore you!" the King answered. "No-one could be more brave, more wonderful, or so perfect in every way."

He kissed her again.

Now he knew that the ecstasy which he was feeling and had never felt before came from Pythia.

It linked them to each other.

It was difficult to think, but he knew this was

not just a merger of their bodies but also of their souls.

How long he stood kissing her the King had no idea.

Then, as if what she was feeling was almost too intense to bear, Pythia hid her face against his shoulder.

It was then the King picked her up in his arms.

He carried her to the big, canopied bed.

Gently he set her down against the pillows.

Only as he took his arms from her did she whisper:

"Please . . . do not . . . leave me!"

"I am not going to," he answered.

He crossed to the window to pull back the curtains.

The sky was brilliant with stars, and there was a young moon among them.

It was shedding its light over the sleeping City.

The King blew out the candles.

Pythia looked at the sky.

She thought the light of the moon which now illuminated the room was a promise. Tomorrow Apollo would again drive across the world, bringing with him the light of day.

It was then the King joined her and drew her into his arms.

It was so natural, so wonderful to be close to him, that it did not even for a second seem surprising.

Nor was it anything she had not meant to happen.

"I love you! God, how I love you!" the King said. "And, my darling, I want to teach you about love."

"That is . . . something I . . . want . . . too," Pythia murmured.

"I have wanted it ever since I first met you. And I thought the love in which you believe was something that did not really exist."

"But now . . . you *do* love me?" she questioned.

"I love you with my heart, my soul, and my body," the King said, "and I think, my precious little wife, we both have a lot to learn from each other."

He knew as he spoke that he would teach her the rapture and passion of love, while she would teach him about the love that was Divine, the love he had thought until now existed only in the imagination of those who wrote about it.

Pythia moved a little nearer to him.

"Teach me . . . oh, please . . . teach me . . . and do not let me . . . make any . . . mistakes."

"All you have to do is to love me," the King said.

Then he was kissing her again, demandingly and insistently.

He kissed her lips, her eyes, the little pulse beating in her throat, and her breasts.

She stirred beneath him, and her breath came fitfully between her lips.

"I love . . . you . . . I love . . . you."

Pythia felt as if they were no longer in the great bed but high in the sky.

The stars were shining not only around her head, but also in her breast and in her heart.

Then the King made her his.

The Light of Apollo covered them as they became one with the gods.

* * *

A long time later Pythia moved against the King's shoulder and he asked:

"Are you awake, my precious?"

"I am too happy . . . to sleep," Pythia said, "and I am just thinking that . . . love is much . . . much . . . more wonderful . . . than I . . . believed it . . . to be."

"I hope I have not shocked you?" the King asked.

"I felt that we were . . . floating above the 'Shining Cliffs' and . . . Apollo was blessing us."

"I am sure he was," the King replied, "and I have never, my darling, and this is the truth, been so happy or so much in love as I am now!"

"You will . . . go on . . . loving me?" Pythia asked. "And you will not . . . find me . . . boring because I did . . . not know . . . about the . . . love you have . . . just taught . . . me?"

The King laughed, and it was a very tender sound.

"That I have taught you is only the beginning, and teaching you, my wonderful, beautiful Bride, will be the most absorbing thing I have ever done in my life."

He paused for a moment before he went on:

"You have not only taught me about love, but also how much I have to do for my country and my people. I need you, I need you desperately to guide me and inspire me, and there will be no time for either of us to be bored!"

Pythia gave a little murmur of joy.

Then the King said:

"I suppose it is because you are half-Greek that Apollo means so much to you, but I too was conscious of his Light when I made you mine."

To his surprise, the King felt Pythia's body suddenly stiffen against his.

Then there was silence until she said in a very small, rather frightened voice:

"I . . . I have . . . something to . . . tell you."

The King looked down at her in surprise.

By the light of the moon he could see her face looking up into his.

Her eyes were very large, and he knew there was an expression of fear in them.

"What is upsetting you?" he asked.

"Because I . . . love you," she said in a broken little voice, "I cannot . . . go on lying . . . and I must . . . tell you . . . the truth."

"The truth?" the King questioned. "How have you lied to me?"

She did not speak, and he asked:

"You cannot say that you do not love me! I know there has been no man in your life before . . . "

"No, no . . . it is . . . nothing like . . . that," Pythia said quickly. "But perhaps you will be . . . angry with me and not . . . love me . . . any more."

She gave a little sob on the last words.

The King smiled as he drew her closer to him.

"Nothing and nobody could ever stop me from loving you," he said. "That would be impossible!"

"Then . . . I will tell . . . you what . . . hap-

pened," Pythia said. "But please . . . before I do
so . . . kiss me once again . . . for you may not
want to do so . . . ever again."

The King did not say that was an impossible
thing to happen.

He merely took possession of her lips.

Now he kissed her possessively, demandingly,
as if he wanted to make sure that she belonged
to him.

He felt the blood begin to throb in his temples,
and once again her body was quivering against his.

He lay back against the pillows, saying:

"Tell me what you have to confess, my lovely
one. I cannot believe it is of any consequence."

In a hesitating little voice Pythia began:

"When Queen Victoria . . . sent for . . . Prin-
cess Aileen to . . . tell her that . . . her daughter,
Princess Erina, was . . . to marry . . . the King of
Vultarnia . . . Erina refused . . . to do so."

This was something the King had not expected.

He turned his head to look down at his wife.

Her fair hair, almost silver in the moonlight, was
flowing over her shoulders and onto his chest.

She was looking up at the stars as she spoke.

He thought her profile silhouetted against the
shadows was the loveliest thing he had ever seen.

"My cousin . . . Erina," she went on, "was . . .
in love with a man she had . . . just met who . . .
came from . . . Peru."

There was a little pause, and the King did not
speak.

Pythia added in a voice he could hardly hear:

"I . . . I took . . . her place."

She felt as she spoke as if the ceiling were falling in and she had thrown away her happiness for ever.

"Then if you are not Erina," the King asked quietly, "who are you?"

"I am her cousin . . . my mother was Princess Aileen's younger sister and my . . . father was an Irish Doctor . . . called Patrick O'Connor."

"And Princess Aileen agreed to this deception?" the King enquired.

"There was . . . nothing else . . . she could do," Pythia answered. "Erina left very early . . . the next morning . . . to board Marcos's yacht, where they . . . were to be . . . married by his Captain. When the Ambassador called in the Queen's instructions, he never doubted for . . . one moment that I was not . . . my aunt's . . . daughter!"

Now, because she was so afraid what the King's reaction would be, tears began to run down Pythia's cheeks.

She shut her eyes.

Then to her astonishment she heard the King laugh.

"Always the unexpected!" he said. "Always the surprise! I could not imagine what you were going to tell me!"

"Y-you are . . . not angry?" Pythia asked with a pleading note in her voice.

He pulled her closer to him.

"Whoever you are," he said, "you are the only person I have ever loved, and now tell me more of this fantastic story."

Feeling more secure with his strong arms around her, Pythia obeyed.

She told him how she had travelled all over the Balkans with her father, how she helped him with the people he cured with his medical skills.

She also explained how he had not actually preached to people as the Missionary Society had expected.

Instead, he listened to their troubles. When they asked for it, he gave them his advice and helped them to be happy.

She also told the King that her name was really Pythia, although she had been christened Erina also.

She explained how her father had dedicated her, when she was born, to Apollo, how he had been sure that she would speak with the voice of the god.

"He was right," the King said, "for, of course, that is what you do. Now I understand why I have thought ever since you arrived in my country you were not human."

Pythia looked up at him enquiringly, and he said:

"You are either a goddess from Olympus who has come down to assist mortal man, or you may be a re-incarnation of the Pythia. That is why the advice that you give me comes from Apollo himself."

Pythia gave a little cry.

"Do you . . . mean that . . . do you . . . really . . . mean it?"

"Of course I mean it," the King said, "and I am very honoured and privileged to have a goddess as my wife!"

Now he saw the fear had gone from Pythia's eyes.

Her body was no longer trembling as he pulled her close to him.

"Whoever you are, wherever you came from," he said, "you are now mine, and I will never, my lovely little goddess, let you go!"

"You are . . . not . . . angry with . . . me?"

"Only astounded that I, a mere mortal, should be so privileged!" the King answered.

He was speaking with a sincerity which made it impossible for her not to believe him.

She lifted up her arms to pull his head down to hers.

"I love you . . . I . . . love you," she said, "and now there are . . . no secrets . . . between us. But . . . it would be . . . best if Queen Victoria is kept in ignorance of who . . . I really am."

"I cannot believe that she will drop in on us unannounced," the King said, laughing. "So, my darling, I am sure you are quite safe."

He touched her cheek very tenderly, wiping away the last tears with his fingers.

Then he said:

"When we are alone I will call you Pythia because I think it suits you, but to the world you are the Queen and that is a sufficient title in itself."

"And you will . . . not mind," Pythia asked, "that the History Books will not be completely . . . accurate when your . . . Family Tree describes me as the daughter of . . . Prince Lucian?"

"I cannot believe that anyone is particularly interested in my Family Tree," the King replied, "except perhaps in the future my oldest son."

There was silence. Then he said:

"When I saw you holding in your arms that baby you had delivered, I knew that what I wanted more than anything else was that you should give me a son, with perhaps some brothers and sisters to play with him."

"Oh, darling, darling," Pythia exclaimed against his lips, "that is what I want to do, not only to make your throne safe since there would be . . . no point in . . . the Russians . . . trying to invade . . . our country, but because I know . . . our son will be as . . . handsome as you, and become as experienced with horses as you and Apollo!"

The King laughed.

"That is what will happen," the King said, "and, my precious, I want daughters who are as beautiful as you, and there is plenty of room in the Palace for any number of children."

He would have kissed Pythia, but she put her finger over his lips to prevent him.

"You are sure . . . quite sure that you are not . . . disappointed that your wife is not as Royal as you thought her to be? The O'Kellys are descended from the Irish Kings, but I very much doubt if the O'Connors are!"

"I have enough Royal blood myself for our children," the King said, "but you, my darling, will give them what you are giving me, a knowledge and a love which is spiritual, and which is accorded to very few men on earth."

Pythia drew in her breath.

"Do you really believe I am Pythia and the Oracle of Delphi?"

"I believe it," the King said, "and also that you are directed, as you have been ever since you came to my country, to people, and above all, its King, for what is waiting for us in the future."

"That is what I want to believe," Pythia answered. "I shall pray, and try in every way I can to be worthy and not fail in the task that has been given me."

"I think the most important thing at the moment," the King said, "is for you to make me happy. I love you, my Precious, I love you with every breath I draw and with every beat of my heart. I also want you as a woman and my wife."

He paused for a moment before he said:

"Have you forgotten, after all that has happened, that this is our wedding night?"

"How could I . . . forget anything so . . . wonderful?" Pythia asked.

As she spoke the King took his arms from her so that her head fell back against the pillow.

Now he was looking down at her and he thought he was right.

She was not a woman but definitely a Goddess, and a priestess from the Oracle of Apollo as she believed herself to be.

Then, because his need for her was very human, his lips were on hers and his hand was touching her body.

The light from Apollo enveloped them.

As the King swept Pythia up into the sky he knew they had found the Divine perfection which all men seek.

It is called LOVE.

ABOUT THE AUTHOR

Barbara Cartland, the world's most famous romantic novelist, who is also an historian, playwright, lecturer, political speaker and television personality, has now written over 500 books and sold over 500 million copies all over the world.

She has also had many historical works published and has written four autobiographies as well as the biographies of her mother and that of her brother, Ronald Cartland, who was the first Member of Parliament to be killed in the last war. This book has a preface by Sir Winston Churchill and has just been republished with an introduction by Sir Arthur Bryant.

Love at the Helm, a novel written with the help and inspiration of the late Earl Mountbatten of Burma, Great Uncle of His Royal Highness The Prince of Wales, is being sold for the Mountbatten Memorial Trust.

She has broken the world record for the last fourteen years by writing an average of twenty-three books a year. In the *Guinness Book of Records* she is listed as the world's top-selling author.

Miss Cartland in 1978 sang an Album of Love Songs with the Royal Philharmonic Orchestra.

In private life Barbara Cartland, who is a Dame of the Order of St. John of Jerusalem, Chairman of the St. John Council in Hertfordshire and Deputy President of the St. John Ambulance Brigade, has fought for better conditions and salaries for Midwives and Nurses.

She championed the cause for the Elderly in 1956 invoking a Government Enquiry into the "Housing Conditions of Old People."

In 1962 she had the Law of England changed so that Local Authorities had to provide camps for their own Gypsies. This has meant that since then thousands and thousands of Gypsy children have been able to go to School, which they had never been able to do in the past, as their caravans were moved every twenty-four hours by the Police.

There are now fourteen camps in Hertfordshire and Barbara Cartland has her own Romany Gypsy Camp called Barbaraville by the Gypsies.

Her designs "Decorating with Love" are being sold all over the U.S.A. and the National Home Fashions League made her, in 1981, "Woman of Achievement."

She is unique in that she was one and two in the Dalton list of Best Sellers, and one week had four books in the top twenty.

Barbara Cartland's book *Getting Older, Growing Younger* has been published in Great Britain and the U.S.A. and her fifth cookery book, *The Romance of Food*, is now being used by the House of Commons.

In 1984 she received at Kennedy Airport America's Bishop Wright Air Industry Award for her contribution to the development of aviation. In 1931 she and two R.A.F. Officers thought of, and carried, the first aeroplane-towed glider airmail.

During the War she was Chief Lady Welfare Officer in Bedfordshire looking after 20,000 Service men and women. She thought of having a pool of Wedding Dresses at the War Office so a Service Bride could hire a gown for the day.

She bought 1,000 gowns without coupons for the A.T.S., the W.A.A.F.'s and the W.R.E.N.S. In 1945 Barbara Cartland received the Certificate of Merit from Eastern Command.

In 1964 Barbara Cartland founded the National Association for Health of which she is the President, as a front for all the Health Stores and for any product made as alternative medicine.

This is now a £300,000 turnover a year, with one third going in export.

In January 1988 she received *La Médaille de Vermeil de la Ville de Paris*. This is the highest award to be given in France by the City of Paris. She has sold 25 million books in France.

In March 1988 Barbara Cartland was asked by the Indian Government to open their Health Resort outside Delhi. This is almost the largest Health Resort in the world.

Barbara Cartland was received with great enthusiasm by her fans, who fêted her at a reception in the City, and she received the gift of an embossed plate from the Government.